A revolutionary approach
to interviewing and hiring
the best

DON'T
HIRE
ANYONE
WITHOUT
ME!

Carol Quinn

CAREER
PRESS

Franklin Lakes, NJ

Don't Hire Anyone Without Me!

Typeset by John J. O'Sullivan
Cover design by Barry Littmann
Printed in the U.S.A. by Book-mart Press

To order this title, please call toll-free 1-800-CAREER-1 (NJ and Canada: 201-848-0310) to order using VISA or MasterCard, or for further information on books from Career Press.

The Career Press, Inc., 3 Tice Road, PO Box 687,
Franklin Lakes, NJ 07417
www.careerpress.com

Library of Congress Cataloging-in-Publication Data

Quinn, Carol, 1960-
    Don't hire anyone without me! : a revolutionary approach to interviewing and hiring
the best / by Carol Quinn.
        p. cm.
    Includes index.
    ISBN 1-56414-577-8 (pbk.)
    1.   Employee selection. 2. Employee interviewing. 3. Employees—Recruiting. I.
Title.

HF5549.5.S38 Q85 2001
658.3'112—dc21   2001042527

ACKNOWLEDGMENTS

This book is dedicated to a wonderful group of people who helped me in so many ways, some perhaps without even realizing it. Extra special thanks to Diane Sears-Campbell, my editor, for being the best. Diane, you were always available exactly when I needed you. Thank you for your faith and encouragement. You have such a magic touch! Also, a special "thank you" to Gene Quinn, who always supported my success unconditionally, and gave of his time even when he didn't have it to give. Further acknowledgment and special thanks are in order for some people, each of whom played a key role in one form or another in helping to make this book a reality: Maxine Jones, Jan Grenell, Ken Ziemke, Jim Hedrich, Karen Priest, Randy Sekeres, Martha Pierce, Debbie Fry, Pam Williamson, Bonnie Pastelyak, Ted Chagaris, Edgar Ochoa, Michael Bruce, Luis Gonzalez, Mark Carpenter, Matt and Cathy Quinn, and of course my mom, Rose Schroeder.

CONTENTS

Introduction

For most people in the corporate world, hiring is just one responsibility of many. For me, it's different. Hiring is my passion, without a doubt. I knew it in college when I had that monotone professor for Personnel Management 101. You know the type. All we saw was the back of his head, because the entire class time consisted of him writing on the chalkboard. To make matters worse, the textbook was dry and had no pictures. All the students complained to each other that this class was a "sleeper." I aced that class. I found the material absolutely stimulating.

From there I went to work for an employment agency. A year later, I opened my own agency. Over the years, I attended every workshop and seminar I could to learn more about hiring. I became familiar with behavior-based interviewing, competency-based selection, targeted selection, and other techniques. The workshops and seminars promised that if I followed the prescribed process, I would hire great employees. But you know what? They didn't always work. Something still seemed lacking in the process. It was hit and miss.

Later, during my years working in Corporate America, a company hired me to revamp its management selection process. A secretary who was promoted to be the company's first official recruiter had developed the existing process. In between the old process being dismantled and the new one being implemented, I became the entire interview process. This meant that I was the only interviewer and the sole decision-maker to determine whether or not an applicant would be hired.

What an exciting challenge this was for me! It would be one thing if these applicants were being hired to work for me, but they weren't. The first time their bosses would meet them was when they showed up for work. Needless to say, this was not your normal selection process, but it was at least an improvement over the old one. And if my hires were good, there would be a lot of praise to reap. On the other hand, if the supervisors were not satisfied with their new hires' performance, I would become the perfect scapegoat.

Well, the good news (and one of the reasons I can write this book) is that the hires were better, turnover dropped, and the cost per hire decreased. One of the best benefits for me personally, and that which had offered the greatest learning opportunity, was the chance to track the ongoing performance of these hires. I could compare an applicant's pre-hire interview with his or her post-hire performance.

Guess what? Those who interviewed the best and even those who had the most skills and work experience were not always the ones who performed in the top 20 percent. And within the group of high performers, there were those who were not the most skilled or the most experienced at the time of their hire. Some of the better job performers hadn't even interviewed well but were hired anyway.

What *exactly* was it that the high achievers had in common that was missing in others, even in those possessing great skills?

The question of this missing piece burned within me for quite a while. During many interviews, it taunted me. I couldn't settle for the interview process the way it was. I wanted to know how to consistently hire well. What was missing? Time passed as I worked in a playground of opportunity, conducting hundreds, maybe thousands, of interviews, day in and day out.

Then, the missing piece started to reveal itself. I began to realize that interviewers are not accurately measuring the applicant's motivation to do a specific job. Most applicants say, "Yes! Yes!" when asked during the interview whether they are motivated—because, at the time, they are motivated to get the job. Sometimes they say anything just to get their foot in the door. But that motivation often disappears after people are hired.

As it turns out, the employee who possesses the best skills to do the job is not always the best person to hire. Knowing what I know today, I'd put my money on the person with the most motivation instead.

PART I

Hiring Attitude

CHAPTER 1

HIRING

Motivating employees is always a hot topic in the business world. As supervisors, we're continuously trying to come up with ways to prod workers to take action, produce more results, and achieve higher goals. We spend countless hours seeking ways to make workers want to perform better. We throw incentives, threats, and rewards their way even if we believe none of these should be required for employees to do the job they were hired to do. Incentives were created to motivate the unmotivated. It is not necessary to motivate the motivated.

Have you ever noticed that the word *motivation* is often preceded by the word *self*? One would think you could just say a person is motivated or isn't. But somewhere along the line, someone attached the word *self* to the word *motivation* to make a distinction.

When you talk about motivation, you aren't automatically talking about *the ability to put oneself into motion*. Not at all. This is where many interviewers go astray. They think all they have to do is assess whether or not an applicant is motivated.

So go ahead and ask an applicant about motivation. Ask him, on a scale of one to 10, how much effort he puts into his work or how important he thinks initiative is.

Or how about an applicant who can talk in detail about the steps she took to finish a tough project. Do you assume she is motivated because she finished the project? The project got done, and that's what counts, right? What if the boss told her prior to the project, "If you miss this project deadline the way you have missed so many others, you'll be fired"? What if the boss constantly had to check up on her progress and push her when she lagged behind? What if this employee argued with her boss, saying the deadline was impossible, there was no way it could all get done, and the boss was being unfair? And what if the employee seemed to spend too much time on the phone or on long breaks? The project finally got finished and barely on time. But during a job interview, this person can brag about how she finished a tough project.

Only talking about the success of the project and conveniently leaving out the details about the boss's push, this applicant probably appears to have been self-motivated. But she wasn't. She had trouble with the "self" part.

If you misdiagnose self-motivation during an interview, you can become the proud supervisor of a new employee who will require your assistance for motivation to do the job. Too many of these people get through the interview process and are hired. These are your low performers. They are the people you *don't* want to hire.

Motivation deals with a combination of influences such as attitude, interest, and environment. Working environments absolutely have an effect on motivation, sometimes for the better and, unfortunately, sometimes for the worse. External motivators such as contests, commissions, employment perks, and discipline/punishment measures are not a replacement for self-motivation. I personally believe they were created to reduce the impact of bad hiring. However, these programs do not fix or change a bad hire.

Prevention is your best bet when it comes to bad hires. The best way to create a motivated staff is to hire motivated people. And hiring highly self-motivated employees begins with assessing them correctly.

MOTIVATION:
THE MISSING PIECE OF THE HIRING PUZZLE

Understanding motivation means tapping into the source of the energy employees invest in their work. Accurate motivation assessment does not always match with what the applicant says or implies during the interview.

Knowing that motivation assessment is the key to hiring well is not a new insight. Determining that this assessment is the reason for most hit-and-miss hiring results, and realizing exactly how to improve it, however, are new ways of thinking.

Imagine how exciting this discovery was to me, a person whose passion is hiring. I understand that most interviewers just want to hire well and don't want to devote their careers to studying interviewing techniques. But for me, discovering the significance of motivation as it relates to the hiring process was akin to being a scientist and finding a cure to a disease—okay, maybe not quite that dramatic, but exciting just the same.

After this discovery, the next step for me was to add specific improvements to the interview process in order to see whether applicants could be selected better. What bothered me for a long time was how simple these changes were. Something that worked this well, and improved hiring this much, should be complicated. After all, if it were easy, we would have figured it out a long time ago, right? That turned out, not to be the case at all.

I came to terms with it being easy, and now it was time to pass along this knowledge to others. It was time to teach it to people who wanted to learn how to hire well but didn't necessarily share my passion for the thrill of the hiring process. This actually became a lot of fun. In so many ways, this information is common sense, and people are so hungry for it. The light comes on in people's heads when they are learning this information. They think of people they know (and even themselves) as examples that reinforce what they are learning.

The beauty of my interviewing method, Motivation-Based Interviewing, is its simplicity. If you're an interviewer, you don't have to throw out your interviewing style or change your process. You can begin using Motivation-Based Interviewing during your next hiring opportunity and see its benefits instantly.

At a recent on-site workshop, an attendee at the director level came up afterward to thank me. He said he had been interviewing for 19 years and admitted he'd never really felt confident that he knew what he was doing when it came to hiring. He said he wasn't terrible at it, but he'd had his share of hiring mistakes. He finally felt he received the training that would help him hire better. He said that he wished he'd had the opportunity to learn this information much sooner.

HOW WELL IS HIRING REALLY BEING DONE?

When we analyze our hiring effectiveness, all we are able to do is examine the performance of those applicants we have hired. We have no way of comparing the performance of the applicants we hired against those we did not hire. In truth, we really don't know whether the best applicant was hired. All we know is how the applicant who *was* hired is performing.

Whether you have your own war stories or have heard the stories of others, hiring mistakes can make you cringe. I have trouble accepting that a bad hire was the best of the applicants and that the ones turned down were even worse or that the interviewer was even skillful enough to pick up on information that would have warned of the impending problem and knowingly hired the poor performer instead of passing. The truth is, bad hires can be prevented.

So often, interviewers lack the know-how to regulate the applicant information they collect during the interview. Unaware, they accept information that is unreliable for predicting future job performance.

That's why Motivation-Based Interviewing is so important. Your success as a manager depends on your staff's ability to perform the job well, achieve results, and meet goals. So why would you want anyone on your team but a high performer?

There are no substitutes for hiring well. Companies can't afford to continue to ignore the importance of educating interviewers on accurately selecting only the best employees. Perhaps you want to rebut and say that in a labor market with low unemployment, where most of the employable are already working, you are lucky just to fill your job openings. During such times, you may have the perception that the real problem is not about the selection process, but more often about having a limited pool of applicants to choose from.

Even in a labor market with high unemployment and ample applicants, determining the best job performer isn't necessarily easier. As the number of applicants for a given job increases, it can be more difficult to distinguish the interview-savvy applicants from the genuine high performers.

Blaming any labor market sidesteps the core problem. Employers are always struggling to keep positions filled due to turnover, and the highly competitive business world never slows down. Those who are employed still keep their eyes open for new or better job opportunities. Hiring high performers is less about the national unemployment rate and really about how to attract those who are ready for a new opportunity and are reentering the job market.

One of my favorite ways to reach quality applicants, which is often missed, is a good in-house referral program. This works well for most types of jobs and is very cost effective. It turns all of your employees into recruiters and reaches their friends, neighbors, acquaintances, and more. You will get a lot of mileage from a referral program if it's done correctly. Of course, you can't forget about being able to accurately identify which of the referrals are a good hire, because not all are.

You should never have to give in by settling for less than the best. Hiring undermotivated employees, skilled or unskilled, and then trying to increase their motivation level makes no business sense. Providing skills training post-hire to those employees who are highly motivated will yield a great return on investment in any labor market.

Hire Well...or What?

How do you make sure you hire the best people? In the Hire Authority workshop *Interviewer Training for Hiring High Performers*, more than 80 percent of the attendees admit that even though they have hiring authority, they have had no formal training on selecting the best employees. Those who did receive some training learned only about the legal dos and don'ts of hiring or some interviewing basics.

Unfortunately, even hands-on interviewing experience doesn't teach interviewers enough. In fact, many interviewers have learned incorrect information about how to identify top performers. This comes with a price tag. The result is either poor hiring or less-effective hiring, and it shows up in your workplace through poor morale, low productivity, absenteeism, high turnover, or other sticky management issues.

One of the most common misconceptions in hiring is that skill level equates to job performance level—*that is the better the skills, the better the job performance.* A lack of the perfect skill set is not an indicator that a person is unmotivated or not a high achiever. Even though skill assessment is important, it is not the most crucial criteria in hiring. Requiring applicants to have the perfect skill set for the job opening at the time of the interview can often mean turning away high achievers.

Skills are useless without the initiative to apply them. The world is filled with people who lack the initiative or motivation to do what it takes to make use of their potential. Some skilled employees may lack motivation; likewise, some unskilled or under-skilled employees may be highly driven to achieve. Hiring well is more than measuring skills. If you rely on skills as the determining factor for hiring, the result can be an employee job performance that ranges from very good to very bad. Skills and motivation go hand in hand, but they are different *and must be assessed separately.*

THE EVOLVING INTERVIEWER

Interviewing and employee selection are steadily evolving and improving. And we still are not finished learning. It was not that long ago that industrial psychologists introduced behavior-based interviewing into employee selection, tremendously improving hiring. Behavior-based interviewing works on the principle that past behavior is the best predictor of future behavior.

The problem with behavior-based interviewing is that it assumes all behaviors are consistent, that they never vary. It infers that every past behavior will repeat in the same way in the future, that every behavior is constant. Behaviors are not quite that consistent. Some people may display certain behaviors only when they think can get away with them. People may be on their best behavior or their worst. This behavior may be something they exhibit often or hardly ever. And all of these factors vary among people.

An example of inconsistent behavior, behavior that occurs only occasionally, merely provides clues for future behavior that is likely to be infrequent. The applicant's normal, everyday behavior is still yet to be determined.

Here's an analogy that may help: Imagine every example of past behavior that an applicant will share with you during the interview as either a green ball or a blue ball. The green balls are symbolic of the applicant's occasional or inconsistent behavior only. The blue ones represent the applicant's most common everyday behavior. The blue ones are most important because they signify behavior that it is likely to continue occurring on a regular basis—in other words, a person's predominant behavior.

If we want to predict how the applicant will perform day to day as a norm, we must be able to see these green and blue balls and not be colorblind to them. Interviewers go astray because they can't see a difference, or they don't know that a difference exists. They assume all examples of behavior will mirror future performance exactly. Without knowing it, they use the information from a green ball to form their hiring decisions. Because this information is much less reliable for predicting future job performance, hiring is inconsistent.

Behavior-based interviewing requires that actual past behaviors are used. This is good because real examples are better than hypothetical responses. But it still doesn't tell us how to distinguish between the consistency of behavior, what behavior is predominant, or how to see the color of the example. Although behavior-based interviewing is more effective than hiring strictly from "gut feelings," it's still not enough to gauge a person's future job performance the way it's currently used.

Pre-employment testing, another advancement in hiring, was designed to assist interviewers in identifying high performers. Not 100-percent accurate, testing is a tool designed only to aid the interviewer, not to replace him in making a judgment about an applicant's rightness for the job. The spotlight is on the interviewer's skill level in selecting the best employees and how that skill level can be approved. To hire well, you as an interviewer must determine the applicant's predominant behavior. If the time you spend interviewing an applicant does not help you accurately predict his future job performance, and do it consistently, then each minute you spend interviewing is a waste of your time.

UNDERSTANDING THE INTERVIEW RELATIONSHIP

To understand why past behavior examples are not enough for predicting future behavior, you must understand the interaction that occurs between the interviewer and the applicant during the interview process. The relationship is a game of control over the job offer. Initially, the interviewer has the control and the applicant wants it. To win, the applicant must receive an offer (but does not have to accept it).

This somewhat interdependent game is called *The Interview Relationship* and it automatically exists between every interviewer and applicant. Let's face it: No applicant wants to be rejected. The applicant is forced into the role of marketing himself by accentuating his positives and minimizing his negatives. To make matters more challenging, the interviewer has a limited time period to gather relevant information in order to make a good hiring decision. Interviewers see only the tip of the iceberg within this time. Untrained interviewers do not usually add value to this scenario. Instead of encouraging open dialogue, they stifle it. If an interviewer shows the wrong type of response, the applicant clams up or amends his story to get a more approving response.

Some interviewers, without ever knowing it, set up their applicants or themselves to fail by their handling of the interview. For instance, an interviewer who talks too much or gives away too much information early on may unwittingly be clueing in the applicant to what the interviewer would like to hear.

Applicants go to interviews on their best behavior and with their guard up, revealing only a small piece of who they are. The applicants are reading books and Web sites offering advice and tips on how to get a job. They use prepared answers and particular examples of past behavior that show off only successes, often without ever revealing any less-than-stellar behavior until after they are hired.

A close friend recently shared with me several experiences she had as an applicant with the popular interview question, "Tell me about your weaknesses." She said the first time she was asked this question, she answered it honestly, spilling damaging information about herself. Later, after reading articles on how to land a job and after gaining additional interviewing experience, she learned to provide answers that actually diverted attention away from her weaknesses. Instead of mentioning that she usually runs late, she stated she is a workaholic who sometimes has trouble juggling everything she is trying to accomplish. She further added comments about how she has improved herself by finding better ways to get more done, all a prepared marketing strategy to avoid divulging her actual weaknesses.

This same friend recently forwarded the Web address of a popular online recruiting company that supplies free information on how to ace interviews. It included all the common interview questions, plus the type of answer the interviewer is seeking. In addition, it listed interview dos and don'ts and suggested questions for the applicant to ask the interviewer. The advice was right on target for what the applicant should do.

The applicants are learning more about getting a job than the interviewers are learning about hiring well.

Being interview-savvy, applicants share examples of their best and brightest behaviors, their best success stories, and their not-so-bad weaknesses. You, as an interviewer, need to determine whether these examples are of an applicant's everyday behavior. But how? Some interviewers have figured out that all high performers, those employees who perform in the top 20 percent, share certain behavioral characteristics and attitudes. Some interviewers try to determine whether their applicants possess these particular traits. Common traits such as initiative, motivation, persistence, a positive attitude, and problem-solving skills are sought in the applicants' responses and behavior examples.

There is a problem with this. The interviewing misconception is that if you find these traits at all present in an applicant, the applicant is a high performer. But these behaviors that are common to high performers are not exclusive to high performers; they're just more abundant or predominant in them. The concept is on the right track, but there is more to assessing high achievers. Remember: Every applicant is either a high performer or pretending to be one. You should not blindly accept every past behavior example as being that of everyday behavior, because it might be an exception to the norm. It could trick you into incorrect judgments favoring the applicant. In other words, that great example of initiative that your applicant just provided could mean he always takes initiative—or it might mean nothing.

CHAPTER 2

ATTITUDE

There is no dispute that high performers accomplish more. But how do they do this? High performers are just ordinary people who are able to produce extraordinary results.

The number-one obstacle that blocks success is *attitude*. Many people fail because they lack the belief they can succeed. They have a multitude of explanations for obstructions in their way that they cannot control. Because they can't conceive success to be possible, they believe it cannot be achieved.

We are just beginning to understand the powerful impact a person's attitude has on work performance, making it probably the most important criteria for hiring. Slowly emerging are hiring slogans such as "hire the attitude and teach the skills." What is *attitude,* and why should we care about it? Attitude is a learned predisposition to respond in an optimistic or pessimistic way based on our thinking. We use our attitude to interpret our life experiences, sort of like looking at the world through a pair of colored eyeglasses. Different-colored lenses will provide different views or outlooks. These glasses, like our attitude, determine what we focus on and how clearly we see. They affect our perspective. Attitude affects how people view and respond to the world around them. It is woven into every part of a person's life. Attitude does not get left at home when a person goes to work—it goes along with him.

Productivity, job-performance quality, initiative, motivation, achievement, and goals are all highly sensitive to and greatly influenced by attitude. There is a direct relationship between a person's attitude toward achieving results and the level of effort that he will put forth. Similar attitudes can be found in similar performance levels no matter what the job entails. How work is viewed affects how much work gets done.

Attitudes are learned, starting early in childhood, when a person figures out *how* to think (usually around age 3 to 5 according to psychologists). At some point, each person establishes a thought process toward viewing difficulties for which they have no answers. This learned thinking becomes established and customary—in other words, a conditioned response or habit.

Even though an attitude can change, it is up to the individual who owns it to change it. I am unaware of a way to successfully requisition permanent change in another person. What a great solution that would be, though: Hire anyone you'd like and then change him or her into what you want.

Attitude change is a personal and willing choice. It is not easy to break the habit of a lifetime of thinking a certain way. The change has to be believed in, desired, embraced, and backed with the commitment of the individual. Without that, permanent change is unlikely.

Even if it were possible for a company to change an employee's established attitude, it probably would be ineffective in both cost and time. Imagine employees going through a complete attitude change every three years or so just to fit their employers' needs. That would be a training department's nightmare!

As a general rule, therefore, the attitude that is hired is the attitude that remains. That means hiring the right attitude should take priority over hiring the right skills, because skills can be changed after the hire.

ATTITUDE IS AS ATTITUDE DOES

If you ask different people to define the word *attitude*, the answers will vary and often will reflect each individual's attitude. It is likely that those people with a not-so-good attitude are not cognizant of it. Even though we all seem to be able to distinguish both good and bad attitudes in others, we have a tendency to rate our own attitude only as good.

Hypothetically, if we did have the ability to objectively evaluate our own attitude and we determined it was indeed bad, I seriously doubt we would choose to share this information during a job interview. The applicants we interview are no different. That means the job of assessing an applicant's attitude is left solely up to the interviewer.

Attitude is thought of as an enigma. Countless human resources professionals have attempted to clarify abstract descriptions of bad attitudes from fed-up supervisors dealing with poor employee performance. We know we want to hire the right attitude versus the wrong attitude or to hire a good attitude and not a bad attitude. But what exactly makes an attitude *right* or *good?*

When we talk about hiring *attitude*, we are talking specifically about *the attitude that is conducive to achieving maximum performance and results.* We're not saying, "Well, I noticed that you have a *bad* attitude, but nonetheless it's still an attitude, so you're hired!"

The attitude we're talking about can compel someone to overcome obstacles and achieve tough results when others without it give up and quit. When this attitude is not present, results lag. The right attitude is crucial for engaging self-motivation, and the opposite attitude has the power to stifle motivation.

Attitudes are made up of thoughts. They can include viewpoints, beliefs, perceptions, and take-aways from personal experiences. They are not required to align with reality. They can become distorted and have the illusion of being correct. Just because someone believes something to be true, that doesn't make it so. Shakespeare said, "There is nothing either good or bad but thinking makes it so." Different people can witness the same event and walk away with completely different perceptions of what happened.

Attitudes affect job performance. The degree to which a company-set goal is believed to be realistic and attainable affects how hard a person is willing to work to achieve that goal. The degree to which anything is believed to be within reach affects output. Any effort expended on a goal that is viewed as impossible is considered to be futile and a waste of time and energy. Common sense says effort cannot make a significant impact on something that has been determined to be truly hopeless.

Both positive and negative thinking have equal power over influencing the perception of attainability or possibility. A person's attitude will determine the conclusion he or she reaches when assessing attainability, and not everyone will reach the same conclusion. Appropriately, *what you think is what you get.* The right perspective has enough power to propel any person into action. A negative, pessimistic outlook hinders performance by discouraging the investiture of effort. This person thinks, *It impossible, so why bother to try?*

In this way, attitude can be the biggest obstacle on the road to achievement—but it also can be a person's greatest edge.

"I CAN" VS. "I CAN'T"

Attitude would be better classified as *positive* and *optimistic* or *negative* and *pessimistic* instead of right and wrong or good and bad. A positive attitude is *active* and a negative attitude is *passive*. This does not refer to the quantity of thought that goes on in a person's mind, but rather the quality, or type, of thought.

Positive attitude refers to the mindset that is optimistic and open to conceiving possibility. This attitude chooses to partake in the most hopeful view of matters and focuses on solutions. It conceives success.

Negative attitude refers to the "I can't" or "it can't be done" mindset that creates barriers and self-imposed limitations. This attitude is unhelpful, discouraging, and problematic. It blocks knowledge and creates mental barriers to prevent success. Given the same set of circumstances, the positive attitude expands to think about possibility and opportunity, whereas the negative attitude squelches ideas and shoots down initiative.

Exactly how do positive and negative attitudes affect effort? Can't people with negative attitudes, fears, and doubts produce just as much or as well as those with positive attitudes? They may think they can, but they cannot.

The mind is unable to act upon thought that is not present. When negative or passive thought is occupying mental space, the focus is on "I can't" or "why it can't be done." There is little or no thought placed on believing it can be done. *Active thought* invokes action through the optimistic belief that the power to achieve desired results *resides within or is controlled by oneself.* It is thought that produces activity or action toward reaching desired results, because it believes it has the power and control to do it. It is thinking that focuses on believing.

Passive thought, on the other hand, is thinking that erects barriers that are *perceived to be beyond personal control* and therefore insurmountable. A passive thinker often claims, "I can't do anything about it because I have no say in it." This negative and helpless way of thinking focuses on why something is impossible to do or is too tough. It focuses on disbelief.

Let's use a computer as an analogy. *Attitudes* are the software programs that operate the computer. Some inefficient attitude programs may not process information effectively and may actually diminish the capability of the computer—like a thought virus. These programs can make powerful computers look weak and not allow them to run to their fullest potential—or to run at all. The program running determines what the computer can and cannot do. Depending on the program, the computer can do a lot, a little, or somewhere in between.

High achievement requires a better program. Attitudes are powerful. They can enable and disable people. The "I can" belief empowers its owner and launches motivation. If action is not occurring, often it's because thought is not truly active in nature.

Active thinkers believe *first* and can visualize the desired outcome. These people achieve results because they spend time thinking about how to do it.

This is the type of thinking that causes action and effort, leaving the passive thinkers disengaged and skeptical on the sidelines. The telephone was not invented first and then conceptualized afterward. The thought and the belief that it could be done came first. NASA did not succeed at putting a man on the moon by believing it could not be done.

FAILURE

Believing that you can is a key part of trying and continuing to try. It aligns with the saying, "If at first you don't succeed, try, try again." Adversity does not force a person to give up; on the contrary, it can be a great educator. Scientists fail many times before they succeed. Failure provides useful information that eventually leads to the cure. The lyrics to the popular song "Never Surrender" sung by Corey Hart state, "No one can take away your right to fight and to never surrender." Failure has occurred only when a person gives up. Quitting guarantees failure every time for every person, without exception.

Who will put more effort into finding a solution: the positive or the negative thinker? Who will accomplish more: the optimist or the pessimist?

The negative thinker focuses on the negative aspects of a situation and often believes the requested outcome is impossible. He also believes his thinking is right. How hard will he work to prove himself wrong? The negative thinker does not believe it is considered failing if he doesn't try.

The positive thinker wants to prove herself right as well. However, right in this case is finding a solution that achieves results. Equipped with the attitude that obstacles and setbacks can be conquered, she puts her energy and effort toward achieving the goal.

On the *Apollo 13* space mission, everything possible was going wrong for NASA. The oxygen was about to run out, and the carbon dioxide filtering system was about to fail. NASA had no way of knowing whether the heat shields necessary for a safe re-entry were damaged during an explosion. The space agency didn't know whether the parachutes required to slow the spacecraft to a safe speed for splashdown would open. There was even a typhoon brewing in the ocean where the astronauts were to be picked up.

In the movie *Apollo 13*, a NASA employee was overheard saying, "This could be the worst disaster NASA has ever experienced." Never giving up, Gene Kranz, the director of flight operations, spoke up: "With all due respect, I do believe that this is going to be our finest hour."

Against the odds, the astronauts returned safely home. You won't be surprised to know that Gene Kranz is the same person who said the famous quote, "Failure is not an option!"

That's the person you want to hire: someone who believes a solution can be found for everything, no matter how impossible it may look.

SHORTCHANGED POTENTIAL

For negative thinkers, hardships and obstacles become excuses. Pessimists shortchange their potential by dwelling on negative aspects of their lives: a bad childhood, personal losses, traumatic experiences, past failures and struggles, fears, and self-pity (often caused by what others have done to them). It is not just past wounds that get attention but also what is currently bad or wrong in their lives.

This pessimism does not exclusively belong to the unintelligent or to those who lack common sense. On the contrary, IQ does not determine attitude. It is sad how many smart people get caught up in negativity without knowing how much it needlessly weighs them down and holds them back.

Non-achievers believe that a particular obstacle or hardship cheated them from their success. They say, "I could have been a better teacher if I had better students." If only they had not encountered this hardship, they could have achieved more. These explanations usually sound convincing coming from a person who is in total belief of them. Although some negative thinkers place their hardships visibly out front, giving the perception of disadvantaged misfortune, others suffer more as silent martyrs. These pessimists often garner polite sympathy from other people, which fuels their negativity.

In reality, these negative-thinking people have given up control. They've made someone else or something else responsible for their failure because they could not see or accept the control they actually had. They tell themselves, "It's not my fault." In the midst of a tough situation, they relinquish their power over it. They believe no one else has encountered their dire straits, or at least none worse than theirs. They feel that the world does not understand this.

The problem with this belief is that it assumes no hardships existed for those people who did achieve results. But the truth of the matter is, *both achievers and non-achievers encounter hardships along the way.* No one leaves this Earth unscathed. The key is in picking oneself back up, dusting off, and getting back in the game and finding a way. It is not obstacles or circumstances that determine results; rather it is the attitude toward conquering them. Obstacles don't make people stop—people stop themselves.

PART II

Motivation

CHAPTER 3

UNDERSTANDING MOTIVATION

We now know it's not skill level that determines job performance. It is motivation level. So how can we hire motivated employees when we barely understand how motivation works?

This section of the book will dive deeper into motivation. It will explain in much more detail *how* people are motivated and *what* motivates them. The focus will be on *self-motivation*.

Interviewers must be able to distinguish between self-motivation and externally generated motivation, which often look no different on the surface. Two concepts, both not yet discussed, will be merged to explain how self-motivation is generated and the degree to which it's generated. Without self-motivation, employees require an outside source to initiate action. That external source is often their boss. High performers, on the other hand, push themselves.

Motivation isn't proved by an applicant's claim that she has it or the fact that she has shown up for the interview. To accurately measure motivation, interviewers must understand how motivation happens. Understanding motivation enables you, as an interviewer, to better determine an applicant's likelihood of producing results. Instead of assessing individual behavioral examples, you assess a purer source of information, one that is unaffected by *The Interview Relationship*. The focus must be placed on accurately determining whether the applicant is able to motivate herself to do the job you are trying to fill.

Understanding the next four chapters is crucial. Until you understand them, do not proceed.

WARNING: THIS MIGHT BE UNCOMFORTABLE

Before moving forward, let me note that some people will struggle with accepting the upcoming information. The information will suggest that all people have control to affect their destiny, that control belongs to all individuals, whether they acknowledge and accept it or not. The information will appear to be unsympathetic and not take into consideration personal situations and circumstances that hinder personal control and job performance. For those not comfortable with this concept, the natural response will be to dispute or discredit it. This response will be their way of protecting what they know to be true.

CONTROL

Control is an interesting topic. There are two schools of thought on it: Some believe that for the most part we have control over our own lives. Others believe our lives are controlled heavily by external powers such as bosses, the government, luck, or current and past events. Who possesses control is a perception that differs among people.

Here's why control is so important in determining a person's performance potential: Along with control comes responsibility—the control over, and the responsibility for, results. A person who is in control is also responsible for his failures. Some people deny that they have control in an attempt to relinquish this responsibility. Giving up control commonly takes the form of non-action. A person can believe that if something is meant to happen, then it will happen without his participation. This person places complete control in "fate" and waits for fate to determine the outcome. He sits back and waits for the outcome to be delivered to him. This, in turn, does leave the actual outcome to someone other than that person, be it fate or whomever. The issue is not that fate possesses control, but rather that control has been relinquished to fate.

Every individual is responsible for his or her actions (or lack of action) and the consequences that follow. Many people do not connect their current situation as being the consequence of their prior choices. Sitting back and not finding a way to accomplish a task is an exercised choice, just as choosing to find a way is a choice. Control is about being able to see all the choices that are available. Some types of thinking reduce control by limiting, discounting, or tossing out options.

What we have learned or chosen to believe about our own control becomes our truth and our perception. The control we believe we either have or lack is our point of view. Denying control does not change the control one actually has. However, if it is not believed to exist in the first place, then in reality control is rendered useless.

What's important about control in relation to job performance is that our actions are influenced by which perception of control we possess. If we believe we have the power to control an outcome, we can choose to take action. On the other hand, if we believe there is nothing we can do, that we lack control, then we view our action as a waste of effort.

A trend among many restaurant chains has been to give servers the authority to give away free desserts and more to satisfy customers who experience a problem. This gives servers the autonomy to make decisions that previously had been made only by management. The servers now have greater control to satisfy the customer. Instead of letting an unhappy customer leave, they now feel empowered to personally be able to make things better. The feeling that one's own actions can make a difference encourages action, whereas the perception of a lack of control does not. The difference can be substantial: keeping customers or losing them.

MISSION IMPOSSIBLE?

Let's look into understanding possibility versus impossibility and how a person determines one over the other. Is there a way to measure or quantify the attainability of something? Is there a mathematical formula that will determine the percentage of likelihood or a mechanical device such as a Geiger counter that will register feasibility? If no such device exists, then how do we know what we should try and what not to bother with, or when to persist and when to give up?

Well, this device actually does exist, but it's hidden in the human mind.

The mind, like the computer program, chooses what it can and cannot conceivably achieve. It regulates our actions. Effort is not willingly distributed when the mind believes there is no possibility of success. Our thinking determines our actions and our actions mirror our thoughts.

In this way, perception actually becomes reality. When effort is withheld, impossibility is guaranteed to become reality. This reinforces the original negative "I can't because it's impossible" perception. Initiative originates from the thinking that desired results are attainable. In the absence of this perception, when the positive "I can do it" attitude is missing, results seem unattainable and performance tapers off. Achievement is a mental game that is controlled by each individual.

PERSISTENCE

Skills and talent go to waste without initiative and persistence. An employee who lacks these will never be a high performer. A lesser-skilled person can produce more results simply by hanging in there. The go-getter has a high degree of both initiative and persistence. The average-performing employee has a lesser degree, and so on.

Initiative, or taking the first step, does not guarantee persistence. Persistence is how long effort continues once motion has started. Without persistence, people quit before desired results are achieved. Without persistence, productivity is reduced—*because you get out of it what you put in it.* Persistence is critical to accomplishment. It is the degree to which action is maintained toward reaching a goal.

Persistence quantifies motivation. Motivation does not happen in just one speed: Go! It is not *all* or *nothing* with no in-between. The amount of persistence varies between people and must be measured to accurately predict future job performance.

Persistence uses energy. This energy requires a fuel source. The fuel comes from the power of a positive attitude that believes results can be achieved. Motivated people have the mental energy to persist; they are energized.

Motivation can be compared to a car en route to a destination. Thought or attitude is akin to the car's transmission. It determines whether the car will go forward, reverse, or even go at all. Initiative is likened starting the car and putting it in drive. "Drive" is the "I can do it" attitude. We must also include some adversity. Adversities are obstacles, such as the detours, roadblocks, dead-end streets, potholes, red lights, and fender benders that prevent us from driving straight to our destination. They slow us down, and it is here where low performers drop out.

Persistence is how full our tank is with gasoline or how soon we will run out of gas. Persistence regulates the distance traveled. And, of course, results are reaching our intended destination.

The more a person truly believes he *can* succeed, the more *control* he believes he has. These are two parts of the same thought. Likewise, the more a person believes he cannot succeed, the less control he believes he has. The less control a person believes he has, the more he believes an external source dictates.

Persistence is not required when control belongs elsewhere. Persistence matches the degree of control a person believes he has. The greater the feeling of control, the greater the persistence. A passionate "I can do it!" attitude produces persistence that is relentless toward achieving results. A half-hearted, optimistic belief produces just a sputter of energy. These spurts of energy produce short-term persistence that will run out quickly. Conversely, an "it's absolutely impossible!" belief produces no perseverance, and sometimes nothing at all.

SUPERPERSISTENCE

Life would be easy if all we had to do is persist straight to the desired results, but that is not usually how it works. To keep things interesting, the game includes obstacles, setbacks, barriers, failures, curveballs, and even naysayers, to name a few of the possible culprits that cause disappointments. All of these and the many obstacles not mentioned are referred to as "adversities."

Adversity is defined as any affliction that keeps things from running smoothly to our desired destination. Adversities slow or block our path to achievement. It is easy to believe you can reach desired results when desired results are easy to obtain. However, when obstacles are introduced into the picture and solutions are not readily available, the "I can" belief is challenged. *Adversities test the strength of an "I can" attitude.* And you can tell a lot about a person by how he handles them.

Adversities draw a line in the sand. Those who are able to get past them are considered to be the high performers. Those who are stalled by adversity do not achieve the same results. *Winners don't quit, and quitters don't win.*

Thomas Edison never would have invented the light bulb without persistence. He didn't just fail a few times; it took him more than 10,000 tries before he succeeded at inventing the incandescent light. The first unmanned rocket exploded or went off course countless times before its inventors got it right. And Abraham Lincoln lost every election prior to being voted the president of the United States.

As Thomas Edison said, "People are not remembered by how few times they fail, but by how often they succeed. Every wrong step is another step forward. None of my inventions came by accident, they came by work." Adversity filters out those people who are not willing to do what it takes.

CREATIVE PROBLEM-SOLVING

Determination to discover a way to achieve desired results is a trademark of high performers. Those trying to achieve results seek solutions. Creative problem-solving kicks in when solutions are not readily available or when desired results seem impossible. It requires a positive attitude. The mental process that engages problem-solving skills includes the belief that unknown solutions are merely answers that are not yet visible. This thinking keeps possession of control and keeps the player in the game.

Solutions are always available, but they often play "hide and seek." Answers can be found when you determine where they're hiding. Sometimes finding them can take quite a while. High performers keep looking without giving up instead of choosing one of the alternatives: waiting until the solution finds them or deciding not to solve the problem.

For high performers, being solution-oriented is part of their thinking pattern. They don't just use this quality once; they use it all the time. It is part of their attitude toward everyday living: Encounter a problem, figure out a solution, and repeat the process.

On the other hand, those individuals claiming victim status or lack of control adopt the mentality that never deploys the mental or physical energy for productive relief efforts. Energy is spent on unproductive behaviors such as complaining, blaming, and pitying. These people become locked in the grip of their circumstances. They want a way out. Rather than seek the best one, they wait for one to find them. Both behavior types repeat themselves.

ENTITLEMENT

Saying you want something is not the same as saying you're willing to work to get it. For many, the preference would be to have success and achievement handed to them. Entitlement is the perception or attitude that a person is owed the desired outcome without being required to work for it. But nothing is just handed out. Vidal Sassoon said it so well: "The only place where success comes before work is in the dictionary."

For the lower performers, their unwillingness to consistently do what it takes originates from their powerless and pessimistic attitude: "Why bother, because there's nothing that I can do? It's impossible!"

Through their eyes, the world operates not on a fair system regulated by effort and persistence but rather on an unfair system controlled by other forces. In fact, effort and persistence are believed to have little to do with success at all.

CHAPTER 4

LOCUS OF CONTROL

From time to time in my life, people have told me that I couldn't do something. I remember one particular time when I filled out a self-scoring career-assessment survey and then shared the results with a close friend. There was a section on working with wood and shop tools. I knew nothing about it, but the test instructions said to rate your interest in each area and not take into account whether you would be good or not, whether you had knowledge or skills, or even whether you could earn a living at the tasks. I rated that area high because it sounded like fun to create something out of wood. My thought wereas that if I took the time to learn, I could.

My friend proceeded to correct me and tell me that I was unrealistic, that I knew nothing about shop tools. He said these tools are dangerous and that I may not be able to catch on. After listening to him, I went back and lowered all my scores in that area. Many years later, I realized that my thought process had taken the path that I could learn or do anything I set my mind to do.

I now realize that not everyone believes this about himself or herself or about others. I've been told that I can't do everything I want to do, but I personally have never understood this thinking. I've been told that my goals are unrealistic, but I accomplish them anyway. I've noticed that these good, well-intentioned people, many of them my friends, really believe what they're telling me. And I also know that I believe I can find a way to make it happen no matter what they think. Achievement starts in one's own mind.

There is a behavioral psychology dedicated to the study of perceived control. It is called *locus of control*. It means the "point or degree of control." It is the study of self-efficacy: the power to produce intended results. It is the amount of control a person believes he has to influence an outcome. It is connected to the amount of participation or effort that his mind will pledge to produce results. Perceived control, attitude, and action are all linked to achievement. Locus of control is the perception of what people believe is under their control—what they think they can do and what they think they can achieve.

One person sees possibility and the other sees impossibility. Both may feel strongly about their position. Both may present a convincing argument to prove their way of thinking is correct. In truth, both are right. Both will essentially work in the direction toward proving themselves right.

Perception of control over attainability is like a doorway with achievement on the other side. The person with the positive, "I can" attitude sees an open door. The opening is symbolic of an available or attainable opportunity. Those who think "I can't" or "it can't be done" see a closed door or no opportunity available.

Locus of control distinguishes each type of thinking. Those who strongly believe *their* actions *can* produce results are *internally motivated*. Those who believe the opposite, that *their* effort *cannot* influence results, are *externally motivated*.

How an Individual Perceives Control

External refers to the perception of events, whether positive or negative, as being unrelated to one's own behavior and therefore beyond personal control. Only through outside intervention do events change. Slogan: "I wish I were luckier!"

Internal refers to the perception of events, whether positive or negative, as being a consequence of one's own actions and therefore potentially under personal control. Slogan: "The more I sweat, the luckier I get!"

The groups are labeled the way they are (internal and external), because of who is believed to be in charge or in control of determining results. Internally motivated people believe that they possess control and are in charge of their results. Externally motivated people see control as belonging to sources other than themselves.

Externals focus outward on what others do to them—an area they cannot control. They don't focus inward on their own behavior—the area they *can* control.

Internal control is not really missing in people who are externally motivated. They just don't see it because they are focused on the external. This perception of lacking control feels like reality—and then it becomes reality. When they don't control their own destiny, someone else does. Outcomes are, in fact, determined by someone or something else when a person relinquishes control. This, in turn, reinforces the original thinking and the cycle repeats.

This is not to imply that people always or never feel helpless. There are those who feel helpless at times but who are able to bounce back by re-thinking their control. Control-deficient thinking eliminates all possible options that involve personal control, leaving only those options belonging to the outside world remaining.

Good and bad external events happen to, and influence, everyone. The difference between people is how much personal control they believe they have to make the most of them or to change them.

Passive thinkers believe that whatever happens, happens, and it is out of their control. If this thinking is correct, then shouldn't that which is believed to be in control—be it fate, luck, coincidence, parents, a boss, or other people—be in control of everyone? Is it that no one has personal control and choice, or is it that some have it but others aren't allowed to? Or is it that everyone has it but not everyone realizes it?

How do you explain the inner-city kid who makes it out of his adverse environment and achieves success when others in that same environment don't? And why do some people succeed in spite of tremendous odds against them and others fail while encountering only minor obstacles?

When an undesirable situation blocks the path, perceiving control is the attitude that *you can* succeed anyway. This "I can" attitude is not always easy to have, but it determines whether action or non-action will follow next.

Externals give up quickly. They quit before others even cause their failure. They feel doomed because they lack control. They have trouble getting back in the game. Control has been given to the external source, which becomes the dictator. The fact that *they* bailed out is not viewed as affecting the outcome. Because they believed that they did not have control over the outcome in the first place, their choice of action made no difference. They were just responding to the inevitable ending.

When I was a little girl, somewhere around age 5, my dad let me steer the car. We were on a dirt road where it was safe. I did pretty well steering straight, but up ahead I was going to have to turn onto another road. This road was coming to an end, and there was a big pile of dirt straight ahead. I didn't think I could successfully steer the car around the corner, and I was terrified I would crash into the pile of dirt. I didn't want to be responsible for that, so I threw my hands up in the air, closed my eyes, and refused to steer anymore. I bowed out! I mentally abandoned control and gave it away.

Every day, people of all ages don't try because they don't believe they can succeed. They throw their hands up or close their eyes. They just let things happen. They say they're not responsible and never know what they actually had the power to do.

As long as I wasn't driving, I couldn't be responsible for what happened. I gave up without trying because I *thought* I couldn't do it. But in truth, I really could've done it if I had just tried, especially with a little help from my dad. At age 5, I was not analyzing the productiveness of my thoughts. Nor do most adults. Fortunately for me, that "I can't do this " thinking did not turn out to be my predominant behavior.

Victim-Status Blindness

Perceived control is invisible to most people most of the time. We can't see what we do with it or where we place it. We don't even think about it, because we're already trained and on autopilot. We don't equate trying, not trying, and quitting with our thoughts about perceived control. We usually don't analyze and connect our successes and failures to how much power and control we feel we either have or lack.

It is much easier to analyze someone else's perceived control than to see our own. Even having knowledge of the topic does not make it easy for a person to see his own control or recognize when he has relinquished it.

The feeling of powerlessness parallels with the feeling of being a victim. The saying, "There are no victims, only those who think that they are" is about learned helplessness. People place victim status on themselves. Their view or focus shifts away from their own control and onto that of the outside world controlling them. Comedian Flip Wilson would always say, "The devil made me do it!"—conveniently shifting responsibility off of himself.

This shifting process is where control is relinquished. Unaware of this habit or an alternative, people become blind to their own control. Half the battle is seeing that we do this and grasping that there is another way of thinking. The other challenge, perhaps even more difficult, is breaking the old habit of thinking.

Lucky for you as an interviewer, old habits are hard to break. That means people are somewhat predictable, which can be useful for you during the interview process.

EXCUSES, EXCUSES, EXCUSES!

Externals let circumstances determine who they are. Events and situations rule their world and then become the excuses for a lack of results. Excuses become habit.

Results and excuses have an inverse relationship. Both are not needed at the same time; it is either one or the other. If results are achieved, there's no need for an excuse. But if results are not achieved, then excuses are offered as the substitute. The fewer results, the more excuses, and the more results, the fewer excuses. Who will gain more results, the employees with more excuses or fewer?

Most excuses are designed to *shift blame away and to shed responsibility*. People say, "It's someone else's fault, not mine. There was nothing I could do about it."

I remember interviewing a young man who wanted to get promoted and move up the ladder. During the interview, he expressed that he thought this was impossible with his current employer and that was why he was job hunting. He said that even though there were promotional opportunities available, the employer was selecting only women. According to him, the company was on a mission to have more women in management. Under those circumstances, a promotion for him would be impossible, he might as well look elsewhere.

Let me tell you what else came out in the interview. He wasn't reaching the company-set goal for profits, but that wasn't his fault. As he explained it, the entire company was down in sales and he couldn't do anything to change that. There were things he could do to improve his job performance, but he always had an explanation for why he didn't or couldn't. If he tried to make improvements at all, he couldn't have tried very hard.

Perhaps this guy is starting to sound like an easy no-hire. But I have to tell you, his image was sharp, he was personable, the labor market was especially tight in his industry, and he had great work experience. Some good companies had hired him, but once he was in those companies, he wasn't getting promoted—and according to him, it had nothing to do with his ability.

It was clear to me that this guy wasn't a high performer. He had one excuse after another for why he couldn't accomplish results. He couldn't even hear how he was coming across because he thought his excuses made perfect sense.

An excuse is different from a reason. An excuse is designed solely to free a person from blame, fault, and responsibility. It is used to justify inadequate results or failure and, most of all, to end there. It is a defense strategy. A reason, on the other hand, is a sound analysis that draws a conclusion from fact. A reason is not designed to relinquish ownership of insufficient results. It is designed to analyze the cause for the purposes of troubleshooting and mapping a solution—in other words, action continues.

The most obvious difference is that an excuse is a replacement for results, ending the need for more action. With a reason, effort continues toward attaining results, and the action doesn't stop there.

We all want to hire someone who will get results and not make excuses.

Anatomy of an Excuse

- Places responsibility on others instead of on oneself.
- Projects negativity.
- Demands perfection in others but is lenient with self.
- Focuses on other people's deficiencies.

VIEWING ADVERSITY

It seems that adults who faced and learned to overcome adversity in childhood are more resilient when encountering the obstacles and setbacks involved with achieving goals. Learning to deal with adversity instead of being protected from it appears to be a good teacher.

Shielding blocks the learning opportunity that is needed to prepare adults for real-world living. This shield cannot be continued into adulthood. Exposure to adversity and obstacles is inevitable. Shielded children grow up without the know-how to confidently and successfully deal with all the roadblocks along the way. Viewing these obstacles as something that can be overcome is the same attitude of control that generates action. It is action that will conquer the adversity and non-action that will succumb to it.

It comes down to accepting the control and exercising the power that we do have to make things happen. The power is ours already. However, not everyone acknowledges it. Some embrace it; others try to discredit its very existence.

How do those who think they're powerless change their thinking? That's the magic question, especially for employers. How can mediocre job performers be transfused with the attitude of high achievers?

Well, there is a problem. There is a device in place to protect the ego.

For a moment, think about how a person who lacks control views life. If you're that person, you're a passenger in life who can't do anything about where you are: You don't possess the control. When people say *you can* change your destiny, it's obvious to you that *they don't understand* the obstacles that exist in your life. If they truly understood, they would not say that.

You'd say, "If I had the power to make things different, don't you think I would? After all, it can be very frustrating living a life where you're unable to change your situation, so have a little empathy please! Those people who obtained success obviously didn't have the hardships that I have had to deal with. It was easier for them."

Imagine the tremendous shock to realize that it's not that the world doesn't understand your hardships but the other way around. Just try to be open to the possibility that it is *you* who does not understand that there is another way of thinking, one that you never learned—a better way. Imagine how you would feel to suddenly learn that you actually had more control than you originally thought and rarely made use of it. One of the toughest parts to deal with would be the realization that all of the times when you mentally gave up without trying, blamed others, and made excuses, *you* could have done things to change the outcome. Your actions would have made a difference, but you didn't bother trying because you thought otherwise.

Often, these people think their sack is the heaviest. While they're making excuses, they never realize that others also carry a heavy load. Realizing that would invalidate their excuses.

Now multiply this realization times a lifetime. The ego-protection device shields us from the tidal wave that would come with owning up to the responsibility for a lifetime of wasted opportunities. In truth, no one sees all the control he or she actually possesses. And everyone denies responsibility that belongs to him or her from time to time. The question is, "How often?" The question is, "What behavior is predominant?"

Anyone can produce results when things are easy and obstacle-free. The true performance test occurs when stumbling blocks and setbacks obstruct the path. When tasks seem impossible, internally motivated employees find a way to achieve results while others apply less action and supply more excuses because they feel they have less control. High performers consistently produce more results because of their attitude toward achievement and adversity.

CHAPTER 5

PASSION: THE SELFISH BOSS

I f you think you have learned everything about motivation, you haven't yet. Hold on tight, because there's still more to come! Suppose you have a job opening where skills are not the deciding factor for hiring—for example, an entry-level job or a job that uses skills unique to your particular company. Or what if you want to hire someone from a welfare-assistance program or someone in the process of changing careers? My point is that a proficiency in a particular skill would not make a difference in who you hired. In each of these cases, a new employee would require training. Would you look for self-motivation, drive, determination, and persistence, the behaviors common to high performers? If you found those in an applicant, would you then be guaranteed a high performer?

Many think the answer is yes. But that is not always true. All of those behaviors are common to high performers, but the problem is that the list is not complete. The presence of those behaviors alone does not guarantee or determine that applicants will be high achievers. So, what's missing, you ask?

Let me use an analogy. Let's say you are internally motivated and you believe you could become anything you want, including an astronaut. But let's say that becoming an astronaut is of no interest to you. Just because you believe you *can* become one doesn't mean you *want to* become one. The same goes for being a surgeon, a police officer, or an accountant, if these careers do not interest you. Should we still assume that self-motivation, drive, determination, and persistence are all there is to high performance?

Imagine for a moment that you are in a car and on a road trip. This trip is called the *road of life*. Are you on the right road, going in the right direction? Do you have a destination? Is this something that you really want to be doing? Are you enjoying yourself? Are you energized or are you exhausted?

Many people get in this car and start their journey before they ever figure out where it is that they really want to go. They jump behind the wheel and start driving in just any direction without first knowing whether it's the right one. Let's say they could go anywhere they wanted to go. Can they say where that is? Are they heading in that direction?

After being behind the wheel for a while, any person is bound to learn some driving skills. That's true whether a person is going in the right direction or the wrong one. How to round corners smoothly, to speed up, slow down, traffic, slippery and bumpy road conditions, and inconsiderate drivers may even become easy to handle. But I'm sure you're thinking, *So what? Driving is driving*, right? Not the case at all, I'm happy to say.

In our training workshops, to make a point, I often poll the attendees to see how many of them have had more than one career. Every time I do this, a bunch of people raise their hands. No matter how they got into their prior professions and no matter how long they stayed, everyone says they eventually got out because they no longer enjoyed it. And they were glad they made a change into something that suited them better. These are capable people who admit they were no longer motivated to do their jobs. They wanted to move into something that they really wanted to do—something that excited them. I wonder how many of the people who don't raise their hands wish they were doing something different.

So what does all this stuff mean—right road, wrong road, loving what you do or not? Why is it really so important that people love what they do, are excited, or are passionate about their work? Does it really make that much of a difference in job performance? The answer is absolutely *yes*!

How motivated do you think a person would be to produce results or an outcome if the outcome was of little or no interest to her? Ask this of yourself. From either angle, the answer is not as motivated as a high performer. But why is this?

Interest produces a connection between a person and her results. Interest makes it personal. Without this connection, there is indifference toward the outcome. It is this connection that personally involves someone. Locus of control is the connection between one's actions and the outcome. Interest is connection between the person herself and the outcome.

The children's song "The Hokey Pokey" describes it well. One part of the song goes, "You put your whole self in, you take your whole self out, you put your whole self and you shake it all about…and that's what it's all about." High performers put their "whole selfves" in.

Connection depends on interest. The greater the interest, the greater the connection. The weaker the interest, the weaker the connection. Connecting or involving oneself in the outcome is what motivates a person.

Driving on the wrong road has a personal price tag. This road never unleashes a person's full performance potential the way the right road does. The rewards are greater on the right road. What's sad is how many people are holding back their potential and are paying a steep price without even realizing it. Somehow they got started on their journey heading in a direction that is better suited for others, instead of one that is right for them. The good news, however, is that there are many who have come to this realization and who have made or are making a course correction. From there, the penalties are lifted and their performance soars.

High performers are ordinary people who produce extraordinary results. And it's not just because of their talent. Yes, something else keeps them going to develop the tools that keep them ahead in their trade. The dedication, drive, determination, focus, and persistence all come from getting personally involved in what they are doing. The key is that they love what they do.

PASSION

Have you ever noticed that we can't completely forget or ignore this inner voice that seems to steer us in a particular direction? And do you know why we feel the most fulfilled when we are doing what we enjoy but don't get that same feeling by doing just anything? Why is it called a "calling"? Is it because the only way to quiet it is to hear it and follow it and because we never feel quite right until we do? Why don't most of us just stay contentedly in our first job or occupation forever? Why is the right career so important? Have you ever given these questions much thought?

Passion can be likened to a wildfire backed with a gusty wind blazing over a field of dry brush. When ignited, passion is a storm that rages inside. It's energy and excitement. It's a fascination, a desire, and a hunger. Passion is a strong inner attraction, a preoccupation, and even an obsession. Passion is a fancy, an aspiration, an ambition, and a magnet. It's all of this and more, but most of all passion is an emotion that comes from the heart.

Passion is held for describing what a person loves. It's a powerful emotion. It is *what* motivates a person to take action. It's *what* a person finds interesting and captivating, not boring or distasteful. It's about pursuing one's likes, not one's dislikes. It is what goals are created from and it's the *motive* portion of the word motivation.

But still, how much do we really know about this part of motivation? Where does it come from? One of two schools of thought is it's just a strong inner attraction to a particular profession—no more, no less. It's a preference that we pick up somewhere along the way. It would seem as if it's something some people have and others do not.

What's funny is that this career attraction happens to correspond with our own natural talents, strengths, personal likes, and interests. It also seems to be something at which we can excel. For those people who are fortunate enough to have an affinity to a specific vocation, motivation is limitless.

Another viewpoint that is held by many (including myself) is that we *all* have a calling in life. Our natural talents, strengths, likes, and interests are our unique God-given gifts or tools that are needed to fulfill our purpose. It's like a specially selected program that each one of us has been given.

What motivates us is a steering mechanism designed to direct each one of us to discover, develop, and dispense our special talents and strengths. In return, we feel the joy and satisfaction that come from doing something we love to do. We are fulfilled. This so-called "purpose" or "calling" is not about everyone becoming Mother Teresa, but about perfecting and fulfilling a niche and having a positive impact on the people we touch along the way.

No matter how you look at it, passion is the powerful influence that pushes or steers a person's motion in a specific direction. For whatever reason it does, it does. You see, motivation doesn't just happen or occur randomly in any direction or every direction. It's a person's passion and interests that steer the direction of motivation. And this direction regulator happens to be the most influential portion of motivation.

Without an understanding of this, it's impossible to truly understand motivation. If you are not comfortable using the word *passion*, if you find it overpowering, feel free to change it to another word you are more comfortable with. Many words work well here, and all refer to that same inner voice that guides everyone. You can use interest, calling, cause, purpose, mission, curiosity, fancy, preference, inspiration, aspiration, dream, desire, goal, motive, and so on. Motivation is *motive* in motion, *desire* in motion, *passion* in motion, a *dream* in motion, and so on.

When you think of *passion*, do you think of someone who expressively waves her arms and hands in the air, who gushes emotion almost to the point of making a spectacle of herself? Can you imagine the low-key, demure person having passion? Demeanor doesn't communicate passion.

Without exception, all people feel passionately about something, no matter how they personally express it. Passion is merely something that holds a very strong personal interest. It doesn't mean a person who is conservative or introverted lacks passion. On the exterior, passion looks different in different people. It should, after all, because the passion itself is different in every person. Passion is what points the way for that person and that person only.

THE BOSS AND THE RULES

What we have done here is use many different ways to describe *degree of interest*. Passion is the highest possible level of interest. On the low end, lack of interest wouldn't be indifference; it would be stronger than that, more like detest or dislike.

You see, those other components of motivation that we talked about in earlier chapters—the "I can" attitude, determination and persistence—have a partner. This partner navigates and steers them, but it does more than that. It has a title. It's the big cheese, it's the head honcho, it's in charge—it's the *boss*! Yes, meet the boss of motivation: a person's *interest level*.

The fact that someone is showing initiative and is persistent does not mean she will consistently apply these behaviors to do everything. If she has no interest of her own in what she's doing and is being pressured by her supervisor, an external source, then the effort will cease when the prodding stops. Remember the analogy about attitude and the open or closed door in Chapter 4? Let's take it a little further. If the applicant sees the door as open, symbolic of an attainable opportunity, the next question is, "Will he choose to walk though this doorway?" The answer is, "If he wants to."

The boss is a selfish boss. It wants only what it wants. If it says, "No, I have no interest," the purse strings are tightened, cutting off the action behaviors. It wants to do those things that interest it, and it wants to do those things first.

A high interest level is like glue. People without this stick-to-it quality often flit from one place to another when a job becomes frustrating. They have no interest to hold them there. Personal interest increases the tolerance level to the frustrations that occur in every job and helps reduce turnover. It makes a big difference when it comes to job performance if a person's heart is in it.

Now, because interest level is the boss and is in charge of self-motivation, it has the prerogative to change and grow. As interests evolve and new interests replace old ones, skills that have been acquired in the past may not correspond with a person's current interests.

People change careers to ones in which they possess no skills in order to satisfy something that's been missing in the past. For some reason we put so much emphasis on skills when hiring and so little on interest level. It's not even uncommon anymore to see an applicant step down in pay and status to start anew in the name of following his interests and seeking personal fulfillment.

It's amazing how a person's energy level and motivation bounce back when he changes to something he loves instead of doing something he finds agonizing. This is because interest level regulates energy. Disinterest drains energy and makes some tasks appear to re-quire more energy to do. Procrastination becomes a common symp-tom or by-product of low interest. Small projects can look like huge mountains to those who lack the interest in them. A high interest level can create an invigorated climber who is ready to scale any mountain to its peak. Interest is what keeps a person energized, engaged, and focused long enough to develop advanced-level skills.

If interest should happen to fade, so will the energy directed toward it. At a very low level of interest, the body may not be suffi-ciently energized to perform the task well. Children stop playing with toys, topics stop being discussed, and books collect dust. Initiative, effort, and persistence are made less available to those areas lacking in interest.

A higher level of interest, on the other hand, increases perfor-mance by dispensing more energy and more of the behaviors condu-cive to achievement. Imagine how much more motivation that passion commands compared with disinterest.

A good friend recently shared with me her excitement about her idea of starting a new magazine. The possibility energized her so much that she would wake up in the middle of the night with ideas about how to make it work. She said that one night after only three hours of sleep she got up and worked on the project some more. She said she felt invigorated and not tired.

INTEREST IN A JOB

If you could do anything in the whole wide world and were guar-anteed not to fail, would you pick whatever you enjoyed doing the most—your passion? Absolutely! And you are not alone. Passion is a magical spark of energy. If you are thinking about underestimating the power of this emotion, just look around. If it is not happening to you, then it is happening to someone you know. There is an epidemic. There is a movement of the masses to do work that is personally fulfilling.

Fulfillment occurs when interests and desires are satisfied. This built-in navigation device guides people toward fulfillment, not away from it. This inner voice encourages the reexamination and the right-ing of incorrect career courses. It's like a divining rod leading us to water in order to quench our thirst. Following the voice inside may not be easy, but ignoring it never produces contentment.

When interest is lacking, it creates a void that yearns to be satisfied. The term *fulfillment* comes from the void being filled. Career counselors and career changes are commonly present when fulfillment is absent but being sought. It used to be called a midlife crisis but now it is happening to us at all ages. Whether it is true or not, it has been said that the fear of aging belongs to those who have not yet found fulfillment and still want to.

Generations back, work was viewed strictly as a way to support the family and wasn't supposed to be fulfilling. You went to work, earned your paycheck, and sought fulfillment on your own time. But we have evolved. In fact, high performers may just be the ones who figured things out first.

A similarity among all high performers is that they love the work they do. Their work and their passion are one and the same. It is less like work and more like a hobby, but they get paid to do it. Their preoccupation has become their occupation, and their vocation has become their vacation. They have found their passion. They are interested, energized, and motivated by their passion. You don't have to take my word for it, just ask a high performer.

As much time as we spend at work, we should be doing something we enjoy. Many are catching on to the good feeling that comes from doing what you love. Imagine the difference between going home after a day of work that was interesting and stimulating and going home after another day of the doldrums. After all, no one made a rule that we could not or should not enjoy our work. The truth is, we touch more people in a positive way when we ourselves are happy.

Happiness isn't something that comes in a paycheck. Many times I have seen applicants sacrifice pay by accepting less, as long as the opportunity satisfies their personal interests and goals. It just so happens that the most effective way to sell a job to an applicant is to talk up those things that personally interest him the most.

You must realize that everyone's interests are different. There is no right or wrong interest or one that fits all. Imagine becoming a police officer or a surgeon if that doesn't interest you. If using a gun or the sight of blood is not your cup of tea, then self-motivation is going to be hard to come by. And it's passion that provokes the entrepreneur to take the leap into self-employment. Imagine doing that without having passion for your new venture.

My friend's father was pushing him to follow in his footsteps, become a plumber, and take over the family business. He tried it for a year before he got the courage to say "no thanks" and then became very successful in the insurance business, something that matched his passion.

Now, the other side of the coin is that the things that hold the least amount of interest go to the bottom of the things-to-do list. For me, that's expense reports. They may be easy. I have the intellectual capacity and skill to do them. It even makes sense to do them pronto so I can pay my huge travel credit-card bill. But I hate doing them! I can't even talk myself into liking them. I understand how this process works, trust me, but knowing it doesn't help. I still procrastinate. I put them off until I can't put them off any longer. That's one part of my job that I will never like doing. Thank God I'm not an accountant; I'd be miserable. And, thank God there are people whose passion is accounting. Now, don't even get me started on taxes!

No Substitutes

When interest level is missing, there is no artificial sweetener to use as a sugar-coating substitute. Companies that experience high short-term turnover, or a number of employees who stay less than a year, often are hiring the wrong match for the job. And this applies whether the employees quit or were fired or laid off. The end results are the same.

I love the opening story in the book *Soar With Your Strengths* by Donald Clifton and Paula Nelson called "Let the Rabbits Run." The story is about a rabbit, a fish, a bird, and some other animals that decide they want to become more well-rounded animals. They decide to go to school to cross-train in areas such as running, swimming, and flying.

You can imagine how the story goes. The rabbit does great in running. It's what he likes to do and also his area of natural strength. He receives lots of compliments on his ability and he likes going to school. He is energized and excited, and he wants to do more of what he does well. Now, imagine how poorly he performs at swimming and flying.

The rabbit goes to his school counselor and says he no longer likes school because he doesn't like swimming or flying. The counselor replies by saying the rabbit is doing just fine in running and needs to work on the other areas instead. The counselor arranges for the rabbit to have two periods of swimming and flying and no running.

When the rabbit hears that, he becomes physically ill! Outside, the rabbit runs into the wise old owl, who consoles him by saying that life doesn't have to be that way. He says schools and businesses could focus on what people like to do and can do well. What a novel thought, concentrating on maximizing someone's strengths, not on a person's weaknesses or dislikes.

The rabbit naturally had the most interest in doing what he enjoyed and also could do well. Top athletes work on maximizing the areas in which they have the greatest potential and the most interest, all of which go hand in hand. It's the exact same principle high performers are using.

Selling a person into liking something does not actually change his or her inner interests. If the job doesn't match what a person likes doing, even trying out the job won't make a difference. If it were to happen that the person did like the job, it's not because someone changed his interest in it but rather that the job matched his interests all along. Whether a person is aware of all of his interests or not, it doesn't change this fundamental principle.

There are simple interviewing methods you can use to assess interests and job match without having to hire someone first. When a person is in the wrong job, both the employee and the company suffer. Sugar-coating a job to make it look like something it isn't, or to look like something a person would enjoy when he actually wouldn't, does nothing other than make a mess for everyone involved.

CAREER PATHS

We know that many factors influence early career choices besides personal interest level: parental and social influences, economic conditions, the desire for money, the ease of the opportunity. The truth is, people do start off in wrong professions.

Instead of one career, it has become common and acceptable for people to have several in a lifetime. Some people take their strengths and move them into a different career field. I know a person who was a professional musician for 10 years and then in sales for 10 years and currently has a very successful career in computer programming. He uses his skills in communication and creativity to excel in his current profession.

That means high performers chasing fulfillment may easily exist among applicants lacking skills. They may be in the process of changing careers and have never done that type of work before. These people are often overlooked in a pool of applicants. There are high-potential applicants out there who are looking for the opportunity and who are hungry to learn. Often, they offer great hiring options in a tight labor market, as long as you can first correctly distinguish who they are and, secondly, train them.

Every day I encounter more and more people who express discontent with their current occupations. In fact, that was the topic of conversation at a recent luncheon. The person I was speaking with said that the only work she has ever known no longer interests her. She was feeling unrest inside. Something definitely seemed missing. She wasn't fulfilled in her current job and was thinking about making a change.

Sometimes it is hard to clarify whether the type of work or the current employer is the problem. This woman wasn't sure which was broken. Figuring this out is not always easy. People often keep the career, switch employers, and continue feeling discontented. It may sound simplistic, but in truth, figuring out the right career can be the toughest part of the journey for many.

People who don't know their interests often keep doing what they have been doing, especially if they have developed skills. It is like being set on autopilot. They just hum along, doing enough to get by, but lacking the zest that kicks a high performer into high gear. These people never become motivated enough to soar to greater heights.

Motivation is tempered until passions are discovered and this energy is unleashed. The existence of the right skill set or the mere presence of the applicant is not an indication of passion or the match between job and applicant. Even good skills and an applicant's enthusiasm are not reliable predictors of a match. Enthusiasm may be only an act and may not last. A match occurs when genuine interest is paired with opportunity.

I think most people generally acknowledge that matching a person's likes and interests with a job is good to do, but it's more than that. People need a playground or an outlet for their interests. When a job becomes the playground for passion, stand back! It's a win-win situation, because both the company and the employee reap the benefits.

Many people reading this will instantly understand what I'm talking about here: the connection between passion and job performance. They are saying, "Yes, absolutely yes!" But, many people are not able to relate to this message quite as well. They don't know this because they have not yet experienced it for themselves. It's not that they aren't one of the chosen few who have been allowed to experience passion. It's that they have never learned how to, or even learned that they are supposed to, bring their aspirations to light and then follow them.

Some people start driving without ever determining their destination. Others don't even know that they're the drivers—they think they're just passengers. If you happen to be a person who has never experienced the powerful feeling that comes from doing what you love, at least know that it exists. No matter what you choose for yourself, however, understanding and assessing passion are a critical parts of hiring high performers.

Whether people have to search deep or just happen to fall into their passion doesn't really matter. Many people do not know just how much interest level affects job performance. This includes many of the applicants you will interview. This means that applicants do not search for jobs only in their areas of interest.

If you forego assessing an applicant's interests before the hire, you're choosing a path guaranteed to produce bad hires. Maximum job performance is backed with passion and cannot happen without it! This being the case, interviewers need to learn how to determine whether the job is the right playground for the applicant's interests, even when the applicant herself is unclear. Do not make the assumption that this is an impossible task, because it is not. This needs to become part of your deliberate hiring formula. It is only when the interest or passion truly resides in the applicant's heart and has the opportunity to be expressed that the highest level of motivation can emerge.

CHAPTER 6

COLLABORATION

This is the chapter that pulls together all the parts of motivation. Up to this point in the book, interest and perceived control have been for the most part discussed as two separate concepts:

1. Interest level is the "motive" portion of the word *motivation*. Interest directs or steers effort. It is *what* motivates a person. A high degree of interest is labeled "passion." It generates energy. The opposite is low interest or "dislike," and it saps energy. Interest pulls a person in and personally involves him. Without interest, the person is on the outside looking in with indifference. To be highly motivated, a person must have a high level of interest in what he is doing.

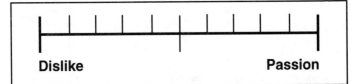

Dislike   **Passion**

2. Perception of control relates to the suffix portion of the word *motivation* or "ation," which means action, such as action toward results. It is part of the behavioral psychology called *locus of control*, which is *how* someone is motivated. A high degree of internal motivation means a person has the ability to put himself into motion. The absence of internal motivation is called external motivation. It requires a source outside the person to initiate action. Locus of control is the

degree to which a person is able to self-motivate. All high performers believe that they are in control of their results. They have an "I can do it" attitude.

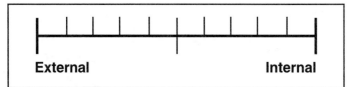

THE BIRTH OF MOTIVATION

Interest level and locus of control collaborate to produce motivation, or "motives in motion." Of the two components, can you figure out which one starts the ball rolling? Is it the stimulus from having interest? Or is it locus of control, the "I can" attitude, the internal sense of control? Here's how it works:

1. A spark of interest awakens and activates the command center.

2. The program running in the command center (a person's locus of control) mentally determines whether action will yield results. If the command center gives the nod, "I believe I can" initiative is activated, effort is expended, and motion starts.

3. Action starts. Interest steers the action in a direction that best allows the interest to be actualized or to satisfy itself—"the selfish boss" is in charge.

4. Interest level and locus of control combine forces to yield persistence. Each of the components is monitored continuously and persistence is adjusted accordingly (increased or decreased) with any change.

Note: Persistence is required to conquer adversities. When persistence is insufficient, motion is easily stalled in the face of obstacles and the current endeavor is suspended indefinitely.

A spark of interest starts motivation. This spark is the stimulus. It is made up of a little burst of energy. Internal motivation is the car's transmission in drive. With a full gas tank of persistence and plenty

MOTIVATION-PERFORMANCE CHART

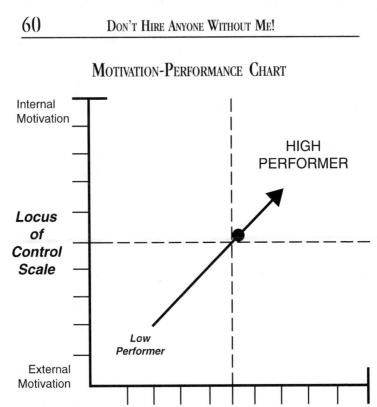

Interest Level Scale

of spark from interest, this vehicle can go far. Interest starts out in command, then locus of control is in charge while processing possibility. Then it goes back to interest, the selfish motivation boss, which directs action to satisfy itself. In the last step, motivation receives input from both interest and perceived control.

THE MOTIVATION-PERFORMANCE CHART

Okay, now can you figure out where different job-performance levels fit into the motivation formula? You must learn what makes a high performer different before you can distinguish this person from the rest of the applicants.

Motivation does not just happen as either all or nothing, or only as highly motivated or unmotivated. For most people, it occurs in degrees somewhere in between. But when you learn about locus of control and about interest, you learn about the two extremes first. You don't learn of the gray areas in the middle initially. Just to let you know, I have never interviewed someone who was 100-percent internally or externally motivated. Every applicant will give both internally and externally motivated responses during an interview. And don't worry if you realize you've also made externally motivated comments. It happens to everyone, including myself. It's not about someone's individual responses that count so much but rather what they dwell on or choose as their focus. It's their predominant response that is key.

The key to assessing motivation is to determine how much control an applicant believes he has to produce results *and* how much interest he personally has to do a particular job. Learning to correlate these components of motivation with job-performance levels helps you not only to hire better but also to better oversee employees after the hire.

A high performer is someone who possesses a high degree of both internal motivation and interest. Conversely, a low performer is someone who is extremely unmotivated because she lacks both perceived control and interest. Both of these applicants can interview well or poorly, have good job skills or not, and be likable or dislikable. Learning to measure motivation will allow you to see beyond a candidate's polished exterior to choose the best person for the job.

PERSISTENCE FUEL

We know that persisting will produce more results. Persistence regulates the distance a person travels. Earlier we discussed how control, particularly the "I can" or "I can't" thinking, has a powerful influence on persistence. But what about interest level: Does it affect persistence, too?

Absolutely! Persistence requires energy to keep the action going. Persistence actually has two fuel sources. Both interest and perceived control fuel persistence. When both are present in a high degree, it is like adding a super-fuel to the gas tank. Combined, they "super size"or magnify persistence. But in actuality they interact differently than that. Think of locus of control as gasoline and interest level as a spark of fire. Without the spark, the gasoline remains a dormant liquid. Similar in process to food being converted to energy within the body, the spark converts the gasoline from mental energy to physical energy. It ignites the gasoline and also keeps it burning. The gasoline is no longer in a dormant state; it is active. It is now energy to be used to fuel motivation. High performers have the energy to persist; they are energized.

The mind doesn't just produce energy; it can take energy away. When people lack action, both perceived control and interest level should be checked. Does the person lack one or both? Has control been relinquished and is a pessimistic attitude in place, or does the person simply have no interest?

Without perceived control, initiative does not happen, nor does persistence. Effort and persistence can also be suppressed by a lack of interest. Remember: At very low levels of interest the body may not be sufficiently fueled or energized enough to keep a person engaged in a task.

Interest is not only the selfish boss that controls the flow of energy to where it wants to go. It also is what converts the mental energy produced from positive attitudes to physical energy. Different types of thoughts, specifically positive and negative, each have a very different and profound effect on our energy level. Energy is needed to fuel action, effort, persistence, and determination. Interest is a positive thought, one that produces energy. This is the energy that is the driving force in high performers and is often lacking in lower performers.

The spark also has the job of keeping the fire burning to fuel persistence. Without this super-fuel combination of interest and a positive attitude, there is no high performance. Without these two components joining forces, there is only average performance or less.

Imagine everyone having the power to be just like Superman— to do remarkable work and soar to great heights. Now think of negative thoughts and the lack of passion as being like Kryptonite, which depletes Superman's energy and drains his power. Some people carry around this stuff, usually without ever knowing. Zapped of their energy, unable to soar, they become merely average-performing mortals.

LEARNING POWER

Some people repeat past mistakes because they never learned from them. They are on a merry-go-round of similar circumstances with different people in different places, but all resembling each other. They never learn what *they* are doing wrong or acknowledge what *they* could do differently. They haven't figured out that they are responsible for or how they have contributed or participated in creating an outcome. Despite that, however, they seem quite clear about what other people have done to them or what others have caused.

Learning from one's own mistakes requires making the connection between one's own actions and the outcome. In other words, a person's actions or lack of action must be seen as contributing to what happens. If it is not seen this way, there is no connection here between the two. The viewpoint then is that the outside world, something other than themselves, something external, is responsible for the outcome. That being the case, there is nothing a person needs to do differently—no change in thinking, behavior, or actions. No learning takes place. The person thinks, *I'm not the one who caused this situation so there is nothing I need to change.* People become stuck where they are, repeating instead of growing.

Sure high performers make mistakes, but they view them differently than low performers do. High performers make the connection between themselves and their results. They don't hold someone or something else responsible for their outcomes even though these external factors may have contributed.

Oftentimes people desire different results, but they keep doing the same thing that didn't work. Ineffective actions, behaviors, and responses must be altered or dropped in order to produce different results. High performers are more effective because they make full use of what they can control: themselves and their own actions. They don't get bogged down or waste a lot of time and energy thinking about what they can't control, ultimately missing what they can do. Low performers have the tendency to think that any change in outcome can occur only if the others involved do the changing. Naively, they often get stuck in this type of thinking.

High performers are less threatened by failures and use them as a springboard to success. They don't quickly place blame for failure off of themselves. Iinstead they look at failure as a learning opportunity. If they are not yielding the results they desire, they say, "What can I do differently?"

Lower performers place the responsibility for learning on their teachers. If they have a difficult time learning, oftentimes they blame their companies for not training them well enough. This shifting of ownership can occur whether they were sleeping in the back of the class or participating. They say, "It's not my fault, I had a lousy teacher," or "There is no way I could have learned in that environment."

High performers may also struggle with learning, but they're apt to take control and do whatever extra they need to do to overcome this situation. They take responsibility for their skill deficiencies rather than blame others for not teaching them.

Learning is affected not only by perceived control but also by the other component of motivation. Lack of interest can also be a problem. What happens when you're trying to learn a topic that is of absolutely no interest to you? Your mind wanders and the topic can't keep your attention or focus. Some people actually cause disruptions in a classroom simply because they're bored.

On the other hand, the opportunity to learn more about a subject of interest sparks our attention and awakens the senses. We transform into full learning mode. Someone who truly is interested and wants to learn a topic will do it, even if it involves enduring hardships.

Teachers and trainers only provide the information. It is up to the individual to learn it. Training effectiveness is greater when those who are receiving the training have both interest and responsibility for learning. Learning reaches its highest peak when people are motivated to learn.

EXTERNAL MOTIVATORS INFLUENCE EVERYONE

There is a variable not included in the Motivation-Performance Chart that also can influence performance. It is the external source of motivation.

External motivators influence everyone—in both positive and negative ways. Adversity can be a negative influence on motivation, and so can naysayers. Demands to produce an income to support a certain lifestyle, demands to put children through college, and an infinite number of other things can be external motivators. Other outside pressures can appear to control and demand a direction that is counterproductive to achieving a desired outcome: "This is not what I want to do, but I don't have a choice" or "I would love to do that for you, but I can't."

What one person perceives to be a negative influence, another sees as a reason to take positive action. An external influence can ignite passion, and, depending on the person's level of internal motivation, it can drive that person to fight for a cause.

The tragic story of a 13-year-old girl who was killed by a drunken driver with a prior record is an example of an external event that motivated. A group of women outraged by this tragedy believed their efforts could make a difference. They were right. In 1980, they formed Mothers Against Drunk Drivers (MADD) to stop drunken driving and to support victims of this violent crime. Today, more than 20 years later, the group now known as Mothers Against Driving Drunk has grown to 100 chapters strong. By educating the public, MADD members have changed the thinking of many.

I'm sure there were those who felt nothing could be done about alcohol-related deaths because they had no control over other people's actions. The issue is believing that our own actions can make a difference and cause change. Those who believe this get further than those who don't, because they try no matter what the circumstance.

There are many other examples of outspoken advocates who stepped into their roles as a result of some negative external event they experienced. The cause becomes their *passion*.

Some people can see nothing positive in a negative situation or in a tragedy. Others can find something good to do even in the worst situation. Some hurdles exist only in a person's mind. They are invented mental nonsense. Regardless, hurdles often do present very real obstacles that need to be overcome. How they are viewed depends on a person's locus of control.

GREW UP BELIEVING

Along the way, externally motivated people didn't learn everything they needed to know about adversity. They missed the section on how to conquer obstacles. Instead, they learned to be stopped by obstacles. They never learned how to persevere. They grew up believing that achievement occurs only when nothing gets in the way to stop it. High performers, on the other hand, produce results despite the obstacles.

Because *everyone* is affected by external sources, those sources should not be thought of as belonging to only select individuals. It's no surprise that most externally motivated people will disagree with this. They use external circumstances as their own personal excuses to explain why they are unable to accomplish results. They view these external factors as belonging only to them and not to those who achieved results. When something is in the way to block success, whatever it is then becomes the excuse. Externally motivated people not only believe that kind of thinking is okay, but they believe it to be correct. When others disagree, it is common to hear these people say, "Well, you just don't understand the situation I am in" or "You really don't know the problems I have that are preventing me from having a lot of choices." Luck often becomes the ambiguous explanation for achievement, and bad luck is used to explain the rest. They do not comprehend how internally motivated people think because they never learned to think that way.

ON-AGAIN, OFF-AGAIN MOTIVATION

Those who are externally motivated have spurts of motivation because of the coming and going of external motivators. As long as an external source of motivation is in a person's life, it can potentially motivate. However, an external influence usually is not constant. When absent, it has little power to motivate. For external thinkers, motivation stops when there is nothing to cause it. It is not sustained: it is inconsistent. It can be sustained only when the person keeps it going himself.

There is good news and bad news with this. The good news is that there is a substitute when internal motivation is lacking—an external motivator, possibly you as a manager. The bad news is that it lasts only as long as you provide the motivation.

On-again, off-again motivation wreaks havoc on results. Waiting for an external motivator to come along to "push start" again reduces accomplishments.

This is why assessing motivation during an interview involves more than eliciting examples of behavior. The individual examples do not allow an interviewer to distinguish between spurts of motivation and sustained motivation. Typically, when we see motivation, all we see is someone taking action. It does not look any different on the surface, especially when you don't know what to look for. It's not the presence of the behavior; it is the consistency or quantity of it that matters.

Those who are internally motivated and have an abundant source of their own motivation will achieve more than those who rely on another source to motivate them. The greater the ability to put oneself into motion, the more motivation there will be.

Every single person can talk about a time he or she was motivated or took action. And because of *The Interview Relationship,* applicants are sharing examples of their best and brightest action behaviors. Those chosen examples of behavior alone do not *quantify* motivation. They do not tell us whether the applicant is internally or externally motivated. They do not reveal whether the applicant had to be pushed to take the action or took it on his own initiative. And they don't tell us how interested the applicant will be to do the job once hired. Behavior examples alone do not tell enough to accurately determine persistence, the key to producing results.

Now that you have a better understanding of how motivation works, the next section will focus on *how to gather* this information from applicants effectively. Bad hires usually do not occur from bad decision-making on the interviewer's part, but from the use of irrelevant applicant information to form decisions. The next section will address information-gathering and assessment. You are on your way to hiring more high performers.

PART III

Gathering
Applicant Information

CHAPTER 7

HOW TO GATHER

It's ironic, when you think about it. All of those inspirational and motivational sayings (such as "Where there is a will, there is a way" or "To succeed at anything, it takes 90 percent attitude and 10 percent skill") aren't usually quoted by the lower performers. Some people can relate to those sayings and live by their philosophy; others think they are just meaningless old wives' tales.

What truly sets people apart is not so much the physical, but rather the mental. I recently watched a television interview with the famous singer Andrea Bocelli. The conversation centered on his New York stage performance. Instead of standing in front of an audience and just singing remarkably, this time he had to act. It included walking over to a bookcase and taking a book from a shelf, moving about the stage and kissing the leading lady, all while singing opera. It does not sound all that difficult until you add the fact that he is blind and had never acted before. His focus was not on the impossibility or difficulty in pulling this off, but on how to accomplish it. Without an extensive vocabulary in English, he quoted the saying "Where there is a will, there is a way"— and because his focus was on finding a way, he did.

But it's not saying the right quote that distinguishes the high performer from the others. If that were the case, the right quotes would be the first thing low performers would figure out to say during a job interview.

I once worked with a director of training who had a reputation for hiring assistants who would stay for only three to four months.

The company, as a whole, had relatively low turnover. Like so many, this director of training did not want to believe that the cause of a bad hire or of her department's high turnover could be associated with her hiring decisions. Oftentimes, interviewers want to attribute turnover to something outside their control such as the work pace, the pay scale, or even the applicant—all of which are issues that can be effectively addressed during an interview. I know it can feel a bit uncomfortable to admit that we have an area that has room for improvement, but if we never open ourselves up to grow, we will never improve and continue to make poor hiring decisions.

Interviewing effectiveness can be deceiving because weak interviewers do have hiring successes. And the best interviewers also have those occasional employees they wish they hadn't hired. But there are many who have made their job much more difficult than it has to be by hiring employees who perform below standards, quit too soon, or fail in some other way.

Making a good hire is not something that just happens. Hiring well is something all interviewers can learn to do. Our next step, in this chapter, is to focus on specific pointers regarding *how* to effectively gather applicant information. The "how" portion addresses creating an environment and using techniques that encourage applicants to tell you more and to tell you things they may not otherwise. You have two choices: You can find out about the applicant before you hire or wait until after—you choose. Getting applicants to talk as openly and freely as possible is crucial for information-gathering, and, ultimately, decision-making. This is why you must create an interviewing environment that encourages every applicant to talk. Learning specific techniques can help you do that.

SHIELD UP AND ON GUARD!

The way the interview begins can have a dramatic effect on information-gathering and on the entire interview. Too little emphasis is put on the importance of starting the interview off right. Setting the stage or creating the best environment for information to flow freely can be key to an interviewer's success. Interviewers who assign little importance to this step reduce their bounty.

Understand that applicants come to the interview somewhat nervous, apprehensive, and with their guard up. Relaxing the applicant lowers his guard. The more at ease he feels, the more the information will flow. A relaxed applicant talks more freely; while an uptight one remains guarded. It is when an applicant feels somewhat relaxed that any safeguarded information tends to slip out.

Here's how it works: A wall is erected in preparation for an interrogation. It's possible for this wall to stay up during the entire interview. The defense begins to lower when there is no sign or reason for apprehension. It is lowered even more when there is a feeling of congeniality and rapport. Getting into the habit of making all applicants feel at ease with you benefits you the most—not the applicant.

Many interviewers think applicants should adapt to the interviewer's comfort level because, after all, the interviewer is in charge of the meeting. So what if the applicant is nervous—that is his issue, right? Some interviewers say, "Why bother with this step?" They jump to the conclusion that a nervous applicant couldn't possibly be a high performer—but they're wrong. Because you as the interviewer have the control, it's easier and more effective if you make the adjustment. A relaxed feeling on the part of the applicant may not occur automatically. You have to create it. This is an important step and should not be ignored. Truly, it should become part of your interviewing process. Don't worry, it's usually not too difficult to do, however. Simply start off by easing into the interview slowly. Give nervous applicants extra time to relax before jumping into serious interview questions. This takes conscious effort, but you will get into the habit of doing it very quickly.

So, how long does it take to relax an applicant? It can take anywhere from a minute or two to 10 minutes or more. It varies because every person is different. Each applicant comes to the interview with a different comfort level. Don't make the mistake of assuming that the most confident one will necessarily do the best job if hired. High performers can feel just as nervous as anyone else can during an interview. And some low performers can be very comfortable during an interview simply because they've had a lot of practice. The goal is to hire the applicant who will do the best job, not the one who just interviews the best.

The best clue to determine whether an applicant has relaxed is his or her body language. Tense or nervous people have rigid shoulders that are held in more of an up position. As they begin to relax, their shoulders slowly drop downward into a more relaxed, natural position. They become less stiff-looking. Hands are another clue. When they are tightly clenched together or fidgeting, it is a sign of tension and nervousness. When the applicant first sits down, mentally note his body language and stiffness. What you are looking for is a change in those signs. It may not be dramatic. Some people will come in more relaxed than others will ever become.

You should look for these clues and adjust *your* style as warranted. Start out with small talk. Remember, some applicants take longer to warm up than others do. A college student or someone who has not interviewed in a long time, for example, may feel apprehensive at first. Adjust the warm-up time on the front end of the interview until you notice that your applicant has begun to relax. This will pay off.

Tips For Creating the Best Interview Environment

- Start the interview with good eye contact and a genuine smile. Smiles work wonders to break the ice.
- Spend several minutes making small talk about the weather, traffic, sports, and nothing controversial.
- Offer the applicant a beverage if possible.
- Interview in a distraction-free environment. Forward the phone to voice mail and leave instructions not to be interrupted. Interruptions make an applicant feel less important.
- Explain the interview format, explain that you will be taking notes, and let the applicant know when he will have the opportunity to ask his questions.
- Provide a realistic time line for when a decision will be made on filling the job. And remember, sooner is better in a tight labor market.
- Treat the applicant with respect. Even if you don't hire her, she could end up being one of your customers or could refer other applicants to you!

Do what it takes to encourage the best flow of information. You may feel you don't have time to coddle a nervous applicant, but what you really don't have time for is a bad hire. The applicant who is not so good at interviewing could still be a good hire. The real answer lies not within the applicant's interviewing ability but rather in his job ability and his motivation to do the job. Personally, I want all the information I can obtain to make my decision—*especially the information the applicant feels a need to guard.* It's very important to give enough time and attention to this interviewing step.

SHOWING NO NEGATIVE JUDGMENT

It is important not only to create a relaxed environment but to keep it. One of the most powerful and highly effective interviewing techniques is the one we are about to discuss. It almost single-handedly evens the playing field by making the interviewer a better match-up with the interview-savvy applicant.

Have you ever been in a line at a grocery store, a restaurant, or anywhere else where you met a stranger and connected with that person? When this connection occurs, it is because the two of you could relate in some way, shared similar viewpoints, or had something in common. As a result, the conversation flowed freely. Now, does the same thing happen when you meet someone and the two of you obviously don't connect or relate? No. This conversation is strained or stifled, if there is any conversation at all. Oftentimes, real viewpoints are withheld in an effort to avoid friction, especially during an interview.

In the interview process, while you are reading the applicant and getting a feel for who he or she is, the applicant is doing the same thing with you. He is looking at you and picking up signals to try to figure you out.

Because of *The Interview Relationship*, the applicant is somewhat forced into a role of pleasing you. Remember that no one wants to be turned down or rejected. Applicants want to receive a job offer and then have the choice to say "no" if it's not what they want. After an applicant responds to one of your interview questions, he is looking at you for your reaction to his answer. Are you pleased or showing disapproval? What do you think happens when he picks up some indication that his answer was good? He feels good. It encourages him to relax and to talk more. He is getting the feeling that the environment is safe and that he can speak up, because the two of you are clicking. He senses you are not judging him negatively, so it is okay for him to share and talk more openly. He lets his guard down.

On the other hand, if the applicant picks up some indication that his answer wasn't what you wanted to hear, then a completely different reaction occurs. Remember that the applicant's goal is to get the job offer. Have you ever had an applicant amend, change, or correct something he said? As interviewers, we all have. The only reason this happens is because the applicant picked up from you a negative judgment. You may not realize that you are outwardly showing your response, but you are. And the applicant saw it. When this happens, it doesn't help any interviewer. It hurts because it often adds only contradictory or confusing applicant information.

When you really think about it, the entire interview is a judging process. In fact, if you don't hire an applicant, that too is a negative judgment. Nowhere is there a rule written that says you must outwardly display any and all negative judgments that you may have about the applicant. It truly is okay if you keep these to yourself, especially if showing it undermines your mission and hurts your results. There is nothing wrong with your applicant leaving the interview feeling good about it. After all, his mission is to show only his best side. Your mission is to gather information from the applicant so you can make a good hiring decision.

Its Destructive Power

A negative judgment or reaction of disapproval during an interview has quite a bit of destructive power. It damages trust, instantly causes the applicant's guard to go up, and undermines your interviewing ability. All of this reduces the flow of information that comes to you. As an interviewer, it is not as easy as you think to conceal your reactions. Most interviewers feel confident that they satisfactorily hide their negative ones, but in fact they really do not.

Think about how easy it is to read the reaction of another person. Oftentimes it's easy to pick up on what another person is thinking or feeling even if he doesn't want you to. All you have to do is look for some outward physical clues. Both negative and positive responses have their own distinctive tone of voice, facial gestures, and even body language. Smiles and head nods show approval; folded arms and frowns send a very different message. The tone of a person's voice and even his eyes often provide obvious clues. As the interviewer, it's difficult to be aware of all the messages you communicate to the applicant with your own body language. Just because we don't speak, it doesn't mean that an applicant cannot pick up on what we are thinking.

People can hone in on the reaction of others—especially when they're looking closely for it, and that's exactly what the applicant is doing. Have you ever had a friend ask you about an interview that you went on? Were you able to pick up some signs about how well you thought it went? What exactly were you picking up on that gave you this impression? If it wasn't something the interviewer actually said, then what was it? This is the same thing that your applicants are picking up from you.

Now, I don't want you to get confused here. I'm not asking you to master a poker face. It is not enough to just conceal a negative judgment. You must go a step further: *The secret is to get into the habit of displaying an agreeing or empathetic response to the applicant's answers.* It can be subtle. A simple nod or smile will generally work. A sympathetic or warm tone of voice works extremely well. It all has to come across as genuine or believable and not phony.

This gets tougher to do on those occasions when an applicant provides information that you happen to find disconcerting. Absolutely *any* negative reaction right here will clam up your applicant just when you want him to tell you more. You especially don't want him to amend or backstroke here. You want him to feel comfortable enough with you to talk openly and tell you more. If he doesn't, he will hold back information to avoid your disapproval. Disapproval is not conducive to a job offer. You have the right to negatively judge, *you just can't show any of it.* Keep it to yourself—it doesn't benefit you!

In one of our workshops, we do a skills-building exercise where attendees get to see exactly how applicants see their responses. From there, we practice having better ones. It sounds simple, but it's one of the most difficult (and fun) exercises of the day. The attendees are the interviewers, and I play the applicant. I give them an interviewing scenario where they just asked me why I want to leave my current job. Once I tell them a shocker piece of information, they have to respond in a way that will allow them to get more information from me. This won't happen if my guard goes up. It must come down and stay down. For anyone who has attended this workshop, you know what I'm talking about. We usually have to go through half a dozen people or more before we get a response that truly would encourage me (the applicant) to talk and spill more information. We want the applicant to confide in us. That's the goal, and have no doubt: It's possible.

In this exercise, I'm not the one who judges each of the responses. The rest of the class does the evaluating. Responses that seem like legitimate comebacks are viewed as suspect in the eyes of the applicant. Even well-meaning, neutral responses with no sign of negative judgment still cause applicants to raise their guard and be leery of giving their trust.

What I want you to realize is that you have to go the extra mile here. That ideal level of conversation that occurs when two people connect is not something that has to just occur or not. As the interviewer, you can produce it. If it doesn't happen naturally, you can create a front or facade that still encourages applicants to talk. This is simply an environment that has the appearance of being very approving of the applicant's answers. For some people this feels awkward and very unnatural, and for others it's easy. You are not changing how you feel; you're just keeping it to yourself and at the same time encouraging conversation. Don't worry if your true feelings differ. That's perfectly okay.

Workshop attendees learn that *how* they ask for more information is as important as the words they choose. If the applicant talks about his frustration with a prior work situation, you should appear to be empathetic and, most importantly, on his side. Smile and encourage the applicant to tell you more without fear of reprisal. Make him think you know exactly how he feels—say, for example, "Yeah, I can understand how you felt. Tell me more about that situation." Come across as if you relate to him and his situation and aren't critical of what he's saying. This will make him feel as if he can tell you anything. It's a highly effective technique for gathering information.

It may seem like a game that you don't want to play, but remember hat the applicants have become interview-savvy. There is a flood of information out there designed to help them to be good at interviewing. Interviewers deserve the same opportunity and must become good at gathering information from these applicants.

Who's Side Are You On?

Sometimes, without ever knowing it, we hurt ourselves and help out the applicant. Somewhere along the way we were given the wrong hiring information or advice. We were told that if we use certain interview questions, we can ascertain an applicant's motivation level. Imagine, for a moment, asking an applicant the following questions. Many interviewers think these questions are effective and enable them to accurately assess motivation. Take a look at these questions and think about how *The Interview Relationship* will affect the answers the applicant gives. How would you answer them if you were the applicant?

1. Are you self-motivated?
2. Do you think initiative is important?
3. On a scale of one to 10, how much effort do you put into your work?
4. Tell me about a project you initiated.
5. How persistent are you?

Do you really think an applicant will admit to not being self-motivated during an interview? How about saying that initiative is not important? Will any applicant say he is below a six or seven on the effort scale? If fact, most will rate themselves a 10 or even higher. Won't every applicant be able to provide an example of a time he or she started something or took initiative?

You get my point. If your applicant isn't a high performer, he's trying to come across as if he's one. In other words, he's pretending to be a high performer during the interview. Similar questions to those preceding can be found in some books on how to hire top performers. These questions give us nothing except perhaps a false sense of confidence that we are receiving reliable and useful applicant information.

Leading the Applicant

Many interviewers make the mistake of providing applicants with too much up-front information about the job or their ideal candidate. This can actually backfire on them and obstruct an unfeigned flow of information as applicants shift their answers to match the interviewer's ideal hire. This is called *leading the applicant* to the right answer. Here's an example of information attached to an interview question that helps the applicant figure out the best answer to give—one he thinks the interviewer wants to hear.

> *Interviewer: "As you know, you are here today interviewing for a cashier position within the theme park. Just to let you know, we provide a 15-minute break for every four-hour shift you work. Sometimes, however, when the park is really busy and the lines are long, your break could be delayed or even bypassed. If that were to happen, how would you feel about that?"*

Do you think even the person who is a chronic complainer will speak up during the interview and voice concerns about missing breaks? No—not if she wants the job. In fact, she may even say she'd be very tolerant of missed breaks because she understands the nature of the business. But after being hired, she'll start to show her true colors. During the interview, the answer she gave was not one that represented who she is or how she behaves. She could easily figure out what the right answer was, so that was the one she gave. She may not be a high performer, but she's not stupid.

Sometimes this leading assistance is offered only to those applicants who are favored and is not offered across the board. It provides no benefit to the interviewer, because it aids in embellishing or distorting information and impedes applicant comparisons. Giving up-front information about the job benefits only the applicant, not the interviewer. Applicants should be required to stand equally on their own merits. And no guidance, accidentally or intentionally, should be provided. If it is the interviewer's intent to explain or sell the job, there are better ways to do this that won't have a negative impact on the selection process. (These will be discussed in a later chapter.)

Because applicants have become smarter in the interview process, interviewers also must become smarter. There is more than one way to effectively gather relevant information from the applicant. The most common way, asking for it *directly*, may not be the best way all the time. Sometimes an *indirect* approach yields an abundance of useful information.

Asking obvious questions straight on can make it easy for applicants to figure out the "right" answer, the answer the interviewer ideally wants to hear. This reduces the effectiveness of the interview and ultimately the interview results. When the interviewer asks any question the applicant is expecting, or even possibly has rehearsed a way to answer, the direct approach has little benefit. "Tell me about your weaknesses" is one of those. Applicants are expecting this question and are ready for it.

One technique useful in information-gathering is asking applicants questions that are less transparent. Unlike direct questions that go in through the front door, indirect questions solicit information by using a side or back door. The reason for the question being asked is not as obvious, which makes it more difficult for applicants to slant their answers. Don't worry, though, we are not going to ask an applicant what kind of tree he would like to be. Just know that, chosen right, these questions have the same power and effectiveness with interview-savvy applicants as they do with those who are not.

We will use direct questions to assess skill level and indirect questions to collect information about what motivates an applicant. You will find that this will more consistently produce good results. (In the next chapter, we will address specific direct and indirect questions.)

All of the interviewing techniques recommended here are highly effective, and this time they favor the interviewer. As simple as they are, they're not known by many interviewers. Managers with current hiring responsibility are making hiring decisions without knowing this information. It seems that if we are able to carry on a conversation and ask some questions, we are considered an interviewer.

Learning how to encourage applicants to talk more openly is a winning maneuver for all interviewers. Those involved in making hiring decisions can no longer get by on what they learned on their own. Interviewing experience alone is an inadequate teacher. Understand that those companies that do not seek additional education will not keep up with those companies that do. Not learning absolutely everything you can about how to hire the greatest employees makes the challenging job of running a department or a business even more difficult.

CHAPTER 8

WHAT TO GATHER

This chapter introduces a simple yet highly effective approach to interviewing and assessing applicants: *Motivation-Based Interviewing*. It is based on the principle that the best way to predict future work performance is to measure the applicant's level of self-motivation to do a particular job. It focuses specifically on *what* information should be gathered or is relevant for this assessment. Information-gathering will concentrate mainly on two areas: obtaining locus of control information and capturing accurate interest level data.

WHAT APPLICANT INFORMATION IS KEY?

To determine motivation, you must separately assess interest level (motive) and locus of control (motion) information. But it's easy. You will find that many of the questions you ask applicants will provide dual information. In other words, one question, or more specifically one answer, will provide more than one piece of information. It's possible to receive locus of control and skill level information or skill level and interest level information from just one question. And these questions probably are not much different from what you are already asking.

The key to determining an applicant's locus of control is to learn how he *responds to adversity*. And the key to interpreting interest level is to learn what interests the applicant by *indirectly* asking about his *likes, skill strengths, and goals.* It is not complicated and should not be made into something complex. What is important is that it's effective.

Critical to both information-gathering and accurate assessment are two factors:

1. Forming effective interview questions.
2. Objectively listening, listening, listening.

First, know that when the interviewer is talking, then the applicant is not. When the applicant is not talking, he is not providing information about himself. You need as much relevant applicant information as you can get to make a good hiring decision. Never is it better to have less information.

You, as the interviewer, must plan your strategy ahead of time. Thinking up questions as you go puts your focus on what question to ask next instead of what the applicant is saying. This isn't good. It interferes with your ability to listen. You cannot focus on both thinking up your next question and listening to what the applicant is saying at the same time. One will lose out. You're bound to miss hearing some applicant information, miss some questions to ask, or perhaps miss some of both. The entire interview becomes less effective than it could be.

You should figure out what you want to ask before you go into the interview, and then you can focus on listening. Write out your questions ahead of time. This will help you to choose the best phrasing that will be the most productive. Then just ask any follow-up questions as they come up.

It's not just listening, it's objectively listening. The word *objectively* accompanies the word *listening.* Do not miss this because it is important. Many people believe that they listen just fine, that they don't need any improvement. They believe that they have no prejudices or biases that interfere with their listening ability or that they do not stereotype or typecast people into groups. Quite often these prejudices sway our thinking and we don't even know it. They can interfere with how we listen and what we hear. When this happens, we lose our objectivity.

Losing objectivity is like wearing horse blinders: We have only limited vision. We have a feeling that we like or don't like a particular applicant, but we can't say why exactly. We can't quite put our finger on the reason. As we interview, the only information we see or hear is that which validates this feeling, and the rest is missed or pushed aside. A lack of objectivity can single-handedly dissolve the effectiveness of any interview training.

It's similar to the "halo effect," in which a small piece of good or bad information overshadows the entire body of facts about the applicant. The results can be that a potentially good employee is thought to be a bad one based on a small piece of information, and the good applicant is subsequently turned away. Or worse yet, the opposite happens. A bad employee is mistaken for a good one and is hired because the interviewer didn't take time to objectively gather relevant information.

Here are some good rules to follow:

- Allow the applicant to do the majority of the talking and focus on listening to what he or she is saying.
- Don't make up your mind too early in the interview process.
- Continue to listen objectively throughout the entire interview until all the information is in.
- Base your decision on solid information and not on a feeling that you can't explain.
- Remind yourself that hiring based on a "feeling" would never stand up in court if challenged.

An objective interview is the best way to uncover the information you need to make a sound hiring decision. If you have a bad feeling about an applicant, and if that feeling has merit, the reason why will come out in a good interview. And if that feeling had no merit, nothing will be there to substantiate it.

Know that this good or bad feeling you get is normal, but also know that it is *not* always accurate. It can be wrong. This means sometimes it will be right but also sometimes it won't be. After years of experience interviewing candidates myself and working with many other interviewers, I don't know anyone whose gut feeling has ever been 100-percent correct—no one. After all, we are talking about predicting the future performance (performance that hasn't occurred yet) of people we hardly know. Don't be closed-off to the fact that your "feeling" about an applicant could be without merit. Conduct an effective interview. Don't go running off on a tangent based on a feeling and lose track of information-gathering.

THE BASICS ABOUT INTERVIEW QUESTIONS

Your ability to listen for the information woven within an applicant's answers will be more important than the questions themselves. But that doesn't make the questions you ask unimportant. Asking poorly designed questions instead of good ones can reap different information from the same applicant. Don't think the information you gather doesn't make a difference—it does. Bad or irrelevant information, or information that doesn't predict future performance, is the reason behind most bad hires.

We will be working specifically on designing behavior-based interview questions. If you don't know anything about behavior-based interviewing, that's okay. It's simple. It merely involves asking interview questions that solicit actual examples of an applicant's past behavior as opposed to hypothetical responses about how he would handle the situation if he encountered it. Yes/no questions are avoided because they yield little to no information.

Behavior-based interviewing is a great information-gathering tool, but most people who advocate it fall short on explaining how to assess the information you gather. Don't worry: We will take care of that by using Motivation-Based Interviewing.

Even though skill level does not determine performance level, many if not most jobs require an adequate set of skills to do the job. Interviewers do best at asking skill-related questions because that is what they have already been doing. The good news is that you shouldn't have to change too much—just refine.

To better understand the questions that you should ask and the information you need to gather, you need to know a little about assessment. When assessing skills, you ask a skill-related question and then you rate the applicant based on his answer. Basically, you ask a question, listen to the response, and then grade it. Assessing locus of control doesn't work that way. There is no single question or answer that will determine an applicant's level of motivation.

Locus of control is determined by using an accumulation of responses. Throughout the entire interview process, applicants will verbalize their perception of control without even realizing it. From the very beginning of the interview to the very end, you should be on the lookout and listening for locus of control responses. By doing this, you step back and take a look at the applicant from a distance and are able to see a bigger picture. You can see things that you normally missed while conducting the traditional interview. Once you learn how to do this, you won't go back to using the old way of looking at applicants.

The majority of the interview questions will focus on gathering information in two areas: skills and interest level. Creating good questions in these areas will be sufficient. These questions will also supply the locus of control information that is needed. Asking skill-related questions is a good and easy way to harvest locus of control information as long as the questions are asked properly. Plus, the applicant does not even realize the additional purpose of the question. That helps prevent answers from being altered.

"THE STAR SPANGLED BANNER"

Let us focus on designing the actual questions. You should realize by now from what you learned in previous chapters that high performers view adversity as something they can conquer, whereas low performers don't. For high performers, it's not "I can't" but rather "how can I?" High performers are shining stars. So let's sing a few bars of "The Star Spangled Banner" in their honor:

"Oh say can you see..."

Okay, that's enough. Why, you ask, did we do that nonsensical exercise? "Oh Say" is the formula for writing effective interview questions that will help you determine an applicant's skill level as well as his view toward conquering adversity, all in one step. It is the *"Oh Say"* method or "O-SAE."

The O-SAE Method uses a set of three questions for each skill that needs to be measured, not just one question.

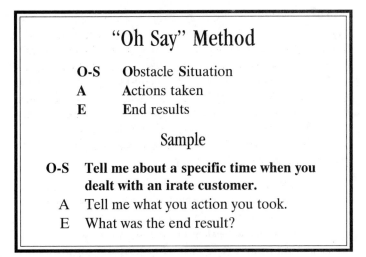

"Oh Say" Method

O-S   Obstacle Situation
A   Actions taken
E   End results

Sample

O-S   **Tell me about a specific time when you dealt with an irate customer.**
A   Tell me what you action you took.
E   What was the end result?

CREATING YOUR OWN GREAT INTERVIEW QUESTIONS

Customizing the question to fit your needs is easy. All you have to do is change the second half, or italic portion, of the first question (Obstacle *Situation*) to reflect a scenario or situation an employee would encounter in the job you're trying to fill—that's all. Begin the question with, "Tell me about a specific time when you..." and then customize the ending for your job opening, such as, "had a crisis concerning one of your software applications" or "discovered that your labor costs exceeded your budget."

Remember that the question must include an obstacle or an adversity. Words and phrases such as "toughest," "most difficult" or "biggest obstacle" can be useful. Both high performers and low performers can perform well when the circumstances are obstacle-free and easy. But when the going gets tough, lower performers throw in the towel. Without an obstacle in your question, you can't see who is who. By inserting an obstacle, you will receive more of a range of answers than you would if you asked about a situation that was easy.

Follow the first question by next requesting the *A*ctions taken by the applicant and finally the *E*nd result. You do not need to customize either of these questions, but you can if you'd like. If it's more comfortable asking certain questions a different way, go for it. For instance, for the *A*ctions question you can also say, "So, what did you do?" or "What steps did you take?" or "How did you handle it?" or any similar variation. Same thing with the *E*nd result questions. You might be more comfortable saying, "So, what happened?" or "What was the outcome?" or "How did it turn out?" All of these are acceptable, and others are fine, too. Here are a couple sample questions:

- **Obstacle Situation (O-S):** Tell me about a time when you worked at improving an employee's poor work performance.
- **Action Taken (A):** What steps did you take?
- **End Results (E):** What was the outcome after one month?

•••

- **Obstacle Situation (O-S):** Tell me about a time when labor costs were too high and why.
- **Action Taken (A):** What did you do to try to lower them?
- **End Results (E):** What was the outcome?

•••

Sometimes an applicant will give an example from when he was part of a team effort and will use the "we" word. I recommend that you not move on from "we" answers until you find out exactly what role the applicant played and his level of participation. To clarify, ask for specific details about what he did. This will help circumvent vague or generic responses, which you do not want to accept. It is up to you as the interviewer to gather quality information.

WIDE OPEN RANGE

A positive attitude toward conquering adversity does not produce happy endings every time. A positive attitude produces the fuel for continued perseverance that's necessary for not quitting. The important issue is the quantity of effort expended—or the opposite: the ease with which a person gives up. Both supply valuable information for predicting future performance.

Failure that involved effort and failure with little or no attempt both provide useful clues for future performance, but each means something different. Accomplishments that include conquering obstacles are a better indicator of a high performer than successes that came easily.

Failure has not truly occurred until a person throws in the towel. Defeat cannot be acknowledged while a person is still trying. For a high performer, failure is merely "success in progress." For low performers, however, defeat is often the uncontrollable outcome. It's the reason effort is aborted.

Understand that it's not failure that's the big issue, it's how much effort was put into achieving and how long that effort was continued. The difference between applicants will be how much detail they can supply about their sustained effort. An explanation can't, and won't, include a detailed account of action taken when action was limited or lacking. It will be one filled with excuses instead. If you understand the differences here and ask the right type of question, the applicant will give you what you need to know but not necessarily what you want to hear.

As the interviewer, you should avoid phrasing questions that retrieve only "happy-ending" results. They are dangerous because they can mislead you and cause you to overrate the applicant. For example, "Tell me about a time when you exceeded a customer's expectations" will elicit only positive answers from anyone and could cause you to rate an applicant too highly.

It's best if you do not ask for a certain outcome or end result, such as a time the applicant succeeded or failed. Leave the end results open in the *O-S* question. Save it for the *E* (or end results) question; that's its purpose. Trust me; It works most effectively that way. You want to create questions that can potentially obtain a full range of possible answers. You will be surprised how mixed the end result answers will really be.

Interviewers quite often don't realize just how poorly phrased their interview questions are. The interview question "Tell me about a time when you exceeded a customer's expectations" is a prime example. It is a behavioral-based interview question, but not a good one. It was being used by a large retail organization that wanted to hire managers who would go the extra mile to "wow" the customers. The intention was to measure customer-service skills, but it requests only "happy-ending" responses. District managers were using this question for years. It is true that some examples would be better than others, but all responses would be of customer service success stories. Does that mean every applicant who answered this question well would exceed customer expectations? No way, not even close!

I had a neighbor who was talking about this applicant he had interviewed for an executive secretary position. He said he knew very early on that he liked this one and just knew she would do a great job. He hired her. Whenever I hear an interviewer say this, the first thing I ask is, "Did you conduct a thorough interview?" He assured me that he had.

To give you a little history, we got started on this conversation because in the past, this particular position had been somewhat of a problem. It had been filled with one person after another who had performance issues, and this time he really wanted to hire someone good.

Well, as it turned out, after two or three weeks on the job, this new employee started showing up about 15 minutes late for work. Then it became later and later. Soon she started calling in sick. He said she was doing more socializing on the job than working. It went even further downhill from there. He admitted that this was one of his worst hires ever. By month three, she was terminated.

He couldn't understand what had happened. How could someone be so good in an interview and turn out to be so bad? He said the applicant did a great job answering all of his interview questions and said all the right things. I asked him to bring home his interview questions so I could take a look at them and see whether I could find the problem or, better yet, a solution.

It turned out the questions he was asking the applicants weren't the type that would allow him to distinguish between different performance levels. They were all behavior-based interview questions, but many of them were phrased to elicit only happy-ending success stories. Most did not involve obstacles. High performers and low performers would be able to answer these questions equally well. My neighbor, the interviewer, didn't know any better.

We ended up having a detailed discussion about the fact that almost everyone can do a great job when it's easy, that the true test comes when obstacles clutter the path. This is when lower performers usually drop out, not when it's smooth sailing. I helped him re-phrase many of his interview questions, and I gave him a few more pointers. From there, he went back to the drawing board to fill this position again.

No surprise, he came back and told me what a difference the questions made. He also added that he felt much better and more confident as an interviewer knowing what information was important and how to assess it. And guess what? His next hire turned out to be a great one.

Improving your interview questions isn't difficult. For example, there is a better way to phrase that earlier customer service question, to determine whether an applicant is likely to "wow" the customer and go the extra mile. Simply change the second half of the first question to include an obstacle, such as: "Tell me about a time you *dealt with an irate customer.*" The key is to phrase the question so it requests specific and actual behavioral examples from a situation involving an adversity. This kind of question is more useful because it accomplishes two things: It measures skills and now it provides locus of control information.

Asking for happy-ending examples is suggestive that only those who have surpassed customer expectation in the past can do so in the future. It does not consider those with high potential and no experience or the impact of training. Questions should be changed so they are able to elicit a variety of good and bad responses from applicants.

PERFECT SKILLS ALONG WITH PERFECT TIMING

Be careful how you think about the "unskilled." Have you ever complained that there aren't enough applicants because the candidate pool has dried up? Remember: "Unskilled" means only that the applicant does not have the skills for the job you're trying to fill. We have a tendency to think high performers are only those applicants who have the perfect skills for our needs at exactly the time we need them. And that if an applicant doesn't have those exact skills at that exact time, then he couldn't possibly be a high performer or a good hire. This thinking is inaccurate. It puts the emphasis on the timing of the skill development rather than acknowledging that skill development is a life-long process. This leaves out all of the future high performers—those highly motivated people who, once they have the opportunity to learn the skills, will outperform the average employee. It does not include entry-level applicants such as students, certain welfare-to-work recipients, mothers returning to the workforce with outdated skills, career-changers, or simply the underskilled. Perhaps our pool of applicants isn't as small as we have made it to be.

If you have an applicant with insufficient skills but the right attitude to achieve, it would be foolish to turn him away if you could train him. Truly one of the best features of Motivation-Based Interviewing is the fact that it can be used effectively on the underskilled.

Gathering Locus of Control Information

We know that the true performance test occurs when a stumbling block or setback obstructs a path. Yes, low performers can and do produce results when things are easy and obstacle-free. Ask an obstacle-free question and you will get a good answer from a low performer. But when a task is difficult or seems impossible, it's the high performer who will find a way to attain results; while low performers more often make excuses and provide reasons for inevitable failure. Your interview questions must reveal the performance level differences, not the similarities.

We have learned that perceived control ("I can" or "I can't" thinking) supplies the fuel for motivation and therefore influences job performance. Responses toward adversity reveal perceived control. To assess an applicant's perceived control or locus of control, just look at how she responded to the obstacles she has encountered in the past. Ask the right questions, ones that include an obstacle or adversity, and just let the applicant talk. You listen. The applicant will verbalize her perceived control through her explanation of her chosen actions. You will be able to see differences between applicants in a way that you haven't been able to see before.

To be effective, an interview should include as many questions involving obstacles as possible. It doesn't matter what the particular question is as long as it follows the O-SAE Method. With this method, applicants will provide many examples of past behavior.

All of these examples are opportunities to see how the applicant viewed and responded overall to obstacles in the past. The examples offer opportunities for the applicant to talk in detail about whether he thought he could and followed through ("I can" attitude) or whether he believed he couldn't and didn't bother to try ("I can't" attitude).

This may surprise you, but both types of responses can be heard from every applicant in every interview. What we are looking for is which one is demonstrated most often. The predominant response is the most reliable for predicting future performance.

The applicant's attitude toward adversity has had an effect on how he performed in the past and will also have an effect on how he performs in the future. Past predominant behavior is the best clue to likely future behavior.

Locus of control information isn't gathered only during skill-assessment. There are many places this information comes out. When you are walking back to your office, when you are relaxing the applicant with small chitchat, when you review the applicant's work history, when you talk about why he left a job, and when you're discussing his goals, locus of control information will come out. The key is listening for it. Using the O-SAE Method and creating the best skill assessment questions will help ensure that you have enough of this information to make a good hiring decision.

INDEPENDENT LOCUS OF CONTROL QUESTIONS

I am sure you were looking for particular questions to use, kind of like a set of test questions you could ask every applicant to determine locus of control. You don't have to be locked in with specific questions. Not being locked in is a good thing. Imagine every interviewer using the exact same questions on every applicant. That wouldn't be very effective. Don't get caught up in that. You have the ultimate freedom to choose the questions you want to use. You can be creative. Multiple interviewers have practically an unlimited number of questions they can use without being redundant.

The key is to create your questions in advance. Type them up and print them out. Create enough spacing between each question to write the applicant's response. If you find that a particular question is awkward or never seems to elicit informative responses, rework it or replace it. Hiring well is about putting in the work on the front end. You can't shortcut it and expect good results on the back end.

Once you have created, tried, and refined a set of questions, that work is done. All you have to do is pull those questions out if the job opens up again. You will even find that there are some questions you will ask most applicants, no matter what job you are trying to fill. Those questions usually are unrelated to specific skills and are more general.

Independent questions involving adversity can be easily woven into any interview for gathering locus of control information. Below are some sample questions that offer more ways to collect applicant responses. When you are creating your own questions, just make sure you apply the techniques discussed earlier.

- **Obstacle Situation (O-S):** Tell me about a time when you were faced with a dilemma or a tough obstacle.
- **Action Taken (A):** How did you handle it?
- **End Results (E):** What were the end results?

•••

- **Obstacle Situation (O-S):** Tell me about a time when you thought something was feasible and others did not.
- **Action Taken (A):** How was it resolved?
- **End Results (E):** What was the actual outcome?

•••

- **Obstacle Situation (O-S):** Tell me about one of the toughest goals that you wanted to achieve.
- **Action Taken (A):** Tell me about an obstacle you encountered along the way.
- **End Results (E):** What was the outcome?

Particularly with questions involving adversity, allow applicants to reference any past experience if they have no supporting work-related examples. It will work just as well.

INTEREST LEVEL

Capturing data about an applicant's interest level is different from gathering information on locus of control. Unlike locus of control questions, which are limitless in number, queries that determine interest level are few and specific.

Before you learn these questions, it is better to comprehend the big picture first. You will not be the first person to assess interest level. Career counselors, mentors, teachers, professional career coaches, books, and tests are already doing it. Now you need to learn how.

In order to truly and accurately measure motivation, interviewers must become mini-career counselors. That's mandatory. It really is simple to learn, and you can try it on yourself.

Do you remember from Chapter 5 why interest level is so important? It's the spark that starts everything.

When a high level of interest is mixed with internal motivation, self-motivation results. Conversely, an insufficient interest level can cause motion to halt. Interests are simple to understand. They are mainly comprised of our likes. They encompass our dreams, our goals, our passions, and our aptitudes—all of those good things. Interests are not those things we dislike such as anything that lacks appeal for us, those things we procrastinate doing, or tasks we find unpleasant, tedious, or boring. Everyone's like and dislikes are different, and that's okay.

I have seen some good managers attempt to rectify performance issues by recommending a change in job responsibilities to ones that better fit the employee. This has good success in the food service industry, for instance, where employees with potential can be switched to a different job. A server who struggles with providing good customer service may perform better in the kitchen or vice versa. This may save an employee from being let go, which is critical in an industry that constantly struggles with having enough staff.

Interest can make the unmotivated more productive. In a tight labor market, inspiring low performers by matching them with jobs that interest them is often worth a try when employees are hard to come by. You can also use this when you're taking over an existing staff that contains low performers who were hired before you arrived. Once you've had time to assess the situation, it may be a good idea to adjust responsibilities.

The fundamental principle career counselors use for assessment is to determine a person's likes, aptitudes or strengths, and goals. Then they match the person with a compatible job. The object is to find a job that consists almost entirely of what the person enjoys. The fewer dislikes, the better. It is a very simple concept: If you enjoy your work, you'll try harder and possibly stay in the job longer. If your job is not something you enjoy doing, then you lack interest and wish for something different, and you don't give it your all.

CAREER FIT OR A FITTING CAREER

For motivation to thrive, it needs a place to be unleashed—an outlet. A violinist without a violin or a diver without water lacks the opportunity to liberate his motivation. It stays pent up.

When a job and a person's interests synchronize, when the two come together, it is called *career fit*. It is when the job's duties and responsibilities harmonize with the applicant's personal interests. The two click. The reciprocating relationship provides the outlet for fertile motivation to take flight and for top performers to emerge. It's a win-win situation.

Career fit is not about fitting into a company or culture, but rather about personally fitting into the job. To find this fit, schools, outplacement services, and career advisers often use assessment tools or tests.

One of the most common is called the Strong Interest Inventory. It does just what its name suggests: It inventories interests.

But it does not stop there. This tool was originally developed in 1927 to assist military psychologists with the task of determining which recruit to assign to which job. It was recognized that a person who likes the job of cooking is different from someone who likes tending to the wounded or managing communications. The many benefits of finding a good match were already known back then.

Now, through computer-generated results, occupations are suggested by measuring people's vocational interests—in other words, their likes and dislikes. Over the years, this assessment tool has been updated and has evolved to keep pace with the changes in jobs. As a personal testimony, I can tell you the Strong Interest Inventory accurately picked my perfect occupation.

You should know, however, that career-assessment tools are just one piece of the puzzle, and most were not designed for the purpose of pre-employment screening.

If you ever want to take a look at people whose passion and career are one and the same, just watch any television program that profiles a high achiever. Oftentimes, the person being profiled will comment that she simply receives recognition for doing what she loves to do or that she feels fortunate to be paid so well for merely following her dreams.

High performers go after their dreams. Roadblocks and setbacks do not cause them to abandon their mission. But it's funny: You rarely hear about the obstacles and hardships they conquered along the way. It's because their focus isn't on that, nor has it ever been. They think about the obstacle just long enough to conquer it.

INTEREST-LEVEL ASSESSMENT QUESTIONS

Okay, on to the questions you need to ask to assess an applicant's interests. We are not going to use the O-SAE Method. Here, we are going to work with using *indirect* questions.

Understand that during the interview, asking the applicant *direct* questions about his or her perfect career choice could get you a funny look, as if the answer is an obvious one.

Let's say for example that you are interviewing an applicant for a financial analyst job you have open. In addition to the applicant having skills, you want to make sure she is motivated to do this job. You want to make sure she enjoys doing this type of work and doesn't find it tedious or boring. So, you ask her straight on, "Is this a job that you would like to do?"

Can you figure out how most applicants will answer the question? If they have any interviewing sense at all, they'll say that they love doing this type of work and it's exactly the job they're seeking. I've even advised job-seekers to say this. It's usually not beneficial for an applicant to say anything other than that. Any other answer would be interview suicide.

If the applicant knows or suspects that this is the wrong occupation for him, he's probably not going to admit it during a job interview. This is especially true if he needs a job.

From my experience, there are many who have learned how to answer this question to please the interviewer. They tell the interviewer exactly what he wants to hear. And, as an interviewer, you can't tell when it's a courtesy answer and when it's genuine, because both responses sound the same.

By using an *indirect* approach of asking questions, you avoid alerting the applicants to right or wrong answers. In effect, you bypass *The Interview Relationship*.

If you were to take a poll and ask people what it is exactly that they'd like to be doing job-wise, not everyone would be able to provide an answer. It's because some people truly don't know. All they do know is that it's not what they're currently doing. Because so many people can't answer this question, the direct approach doesn't always work well for assessing *what* motivates an applicant.

When a career counselor starts working with a new person, neither one has any answers yet. Whether the career counselor uses a test or verbally asks questions, the goal is to get more information. And so is the goal of the *indirect* approach. It is simply a method of inquiry. You can get a pretty good idea about what a good or bad job match would be just by asking a few questions and learning about the applicant's likes and dislikes.

When you like a job, it's because you like what you are doing on that job. And motivation is affected by whether a person likes or dislikes what he is doing. One of the greatest benefits of using *indirect* questions to assess an applicant's motivation is that it doesn't require the applicant to know exactly what would make a good career fit for himself. The *indirect* approach works equally well when an applicant knows and shares this information and also when he doesn't.

The questions used to determine an applicant's interests will center around his likes, strengths, and goals. But for the purpose of comparison, it's also useful to determine the opposite information, such as dislikes and weaknesses.

For the questions that follow, remember I promised that becoming a mini-version of a career counselor would not be difficult. There are only five questions, and they're easy. They don't take very long to ask. There are even a couple of very powerful locus of control questions that you can weave in.

Likes and Dislikes Questions

1. Out of the jobs you've had, which was your favorite? Why?

2. Which one was your least favorite? Why?

Strengths and Weaknesses Questions

3. On your last performance evaluation, in which three areas were you rated the highest?

4. On your last performance evaluation, tell me the two areas in which you received the lowest rating and needed improvement.

Goal Questions

5. Tell me about your career goals for the next two to five years.

Let's talk about these questions. There's not much to add to the first two. They are fairly self-explanatory and need no special instructions. I am, however, going to provide you with a couple of options to these questions. I personally like the original set because I find they work the best for me. But use the ones that work the best for you.

-   On your last job (or current job), what were your favorite tasks? And least favorite?

-   If you could change one thing about your last job, what would it be? What one thing wouldn't you change?

For questions 3 and 4, the strengths and weaknesses questions, there are some guidelines. First, always ask about the applicant's strengths first. Ask for three. Then give him time to brag. This will make him feel confident. When you are ready to follow up with the question about weaknesses, downplay it. Make it seem as if you really don't care about the information, that you already like the applicant but you have to ask these questions as a formality. Don't say that, but try to come across that way. That's why you are asking for only two weaknesses. I joke around and sometimes say that I'm not sure of the current politically correct term for "weaknesses" now because it keeps changing, and that I think it's now "areas of opportunity." Usually the applicant chuckles.

The reason you base it on the applicant's last performance evaluation is because that makes the information less subjective. The applicant should have a copy of that evaluation, even though you are not going to ask for it. Also, a reference check with a prior boss may substantiate what the applicant says. So he is put on the spot to provide an accurate answer and one that is less prepared and canned.

If there has not been a performance evaluation in the past year or so, rephrase the question and ask that if his supervisor were to give an evaluation today, what would be the applicant's three strongest areas, followed by the two weakest. I find those questions work just as well.

There are a couple wonderful locus of control questions you can insert, and here is one of them. I would not bother to recommend these if they weren't so highly effective. You'll want to try them out. After you ask question 4 about the applicant's weaknesses, follow it with this question:

> *What, if any, work have you done to improve upon your weaknesses?*

There are usually only two very clear types of responses that come from this question. Give it a try; you'll see what I'm talking about. You'll either get "I can't" and why answers or "Let me tell you what I've done" followed with specific details. Applicants will say something such as, "I haven't been given the opportunity to work on my weakness because the boss keeps piling more on me," or will say, "Even though my job didn't require me to do this, I took a night class to brush up on my accounting skills."

For question 5, the goals question, you should focus on career- or business-related goals. Do not extend the period of time out more than five years or the question will lose its effectiveness, because most people are focused on accomplishing what is immediately ahead of them. Here is where you can add one more locus of control question. After asking question #5, follow up with this one:

What steps, if any, have you taken toward reaching those goals?

Once again, it's common to get one of two types of answers here. Because everyone has dreams, most applicants will state a specific goal of some kind. It's what comes after that's important. Applicants are either going to explain what's preventing them from making progress and will say something such as, "Well, I have so much going on right now with everyone leaning on me to handle all of these responsibilities, it's impossible to work on my goals right now." Or they'll say something such as, "Although I haven't made much progress, I have put together a plan that outlines exactly what steps I need to take and I have attached a timeframe to each. I have called the local college and they are sending me the paperwork to enroll in classes this fall."

These questions do not need to be asked at any specific time during the interview. My preference, however, is to group them the way they are here and ask them toward the end of the interview. Whatever sequence you choose, consistency will build habit. Established interviewing patterns enable interviewers to concentrate on evaluating the applicants.

As the interviewer, you are responsible for your interviews and liable for the applicant information that you collect. You must know what information you need going into the interview and also how to obtain it. Keep this chapter's information fresh in your head, because in the next chapter we are moving on to assessment.

PART IV

Putting It All Together

CHAPTER 9

ASSESSING LOCUS OF CONTROL

So far, you have learned much about *attitudes*, which are composed of many thoughts and have a very real impact on job performance. Attitudes vary among applicants. Some attitudes are conducive to motivation; others have the opposite effect and actually stifle it. In the previous two chapters, you learned what information to gather and the best ways to get it even from the most interview-savvy applicants.

Now you're ready to learn how to assess this information. We are going to start with locus of control. This chapter is devoted to just that: determining whether an applicant is more internally or externally motivated. Is his attitude one that is more conducive to overcoming obstacles in order to achieve results or is it one that believes many obstacles are insurmountable and beyond solution? The next chapter will address assessing the applicant's interest level in doing a job. And from there, you can make the decision to hire or not to hire.

Up to this point, I have addressed the components of motivation (locus of control and interest level) separately. This is because each component is evaluated differently, by different methods and by using different types of questions, and therefore must be assessed differently. Even though they are very different, it is only when they come together that a high performer emerges. Performance levels decline proportionately as the quantity of either one or both of these components decreases.

THINKING VARIES—PERFORMANCE VARIES

Realize that a person's perceptions, which are made up of his thoughts and beliefs, do not always coincide with reality. However, each person usually feels as if his perceptions are reality. It's the people who have the positive attitude that grasp actual possibility and the most accurate perception of reality and not the ones who believe their negative thinking is realistic. I know many pessimists will disagree with this. But they are not the ones turning lemons into lemonade.

I'm sure you will agree with me when I say there is more than one way of thinking and more than one way to view a circumstance. Although one person believes something is impossible, another believes that very same thing can and will happen. Both cannot be correct. It is either possible or it isn't. Something can't be both impossible and possible at the same time, right?

So which type of thinking, positive or negative, perceiving control or not perceiving it, is more accurate or corresponds closest to reality? Let's look at some of the things that were thought to be impossible in the past, which really were not. The building of the Golden Gate Bridge broke records thought to be architecturally impossible. Running the four-minute mile, once viewed as being physically impossible, wasn't. How about the pyramids, man in flight, moonwalks, radio, heart transplants, microwave ovens, laptop computers, and cell phones that ring no matter where we are? You get the picture.

Those who believe they can achieve results parallel most closely with reality, not the other way around. The person who cannot conceive all that can be achieved is the one who is disconnected from the truth. The person who truly thinks he can't, believing that he lacks control or power, causes his perception to become his truth or reality.

When a person disconnects himself from having control over a situation and takes no responsibility for getting into it or for getting out of it, he inevitably does very little. Even though he desires certain end results, he believes he lacks the power to do anything about it. He thinks he can't. Because his effort and persistence are not believed to make any difference, he withholds them. When people release personal control, they stop being the producers of outcomes. They become the passengers in life, allowing the external world to do the driving and to determine what happens. These people wait for obstacles to be removed for them because they believe they're not the ones in control. In their minds, there is no connection between their effort and the results.

The difference is not that the low performer actually lacks control to produce results and that the high performer has it. Not at all! By perceiving control, the high performer simply believes that expending the effort has the potential or at least a chance of paying off, so she tries. If desired results are going to happen, they happen when a person tries and not when she doesn't.

The distinction is that the low performer has relinquished his control within his own thought process and cannot see any payoff being possible. It's a way of thinking or a perception that varies among different levels of high performers and low performers. And because people's thinking does vary and because this variance is visible during an interview, interviewers can evaluate future performance based on perceived control information.

Understand one more thing regarding the low performer's thinking: If obstacles and excuses were no longer accepted as valid reasons for certain outcomes, then each person would be responsible for his or her own outcomes or the lack of them. Outcomes would be the product of personal choice and effort. Do you really think the lower performers, those people who have clung to excuses, want to hear this or are willing to accept it? No way! They want to hold onto their way of thinking because it's comfortable, it's the path of least resistance, and it provides them with an explanation. The behavior repeats and has a pattern because the thinking stays the same.

WHY MOTIVATION-BASED INTERVIEWING WORKS

Motivation-Based Interviewing looks at an applicant's attitude toward conquering obstacles. It looks for (and uses) predominant behavior to predict future behavior. Many interviewers want to predict an applicant's future performance by focusing on his past track record of results. This isn't always effective and is not recommended. Reviewing results only looks at the ending and doesn't look at the attitude or thought process behind the scenes. Motivation-Based Interviewing looks at how the applicant got there.

Assessing only results often reduces the pool of applicants by eliminating college students, career-changers, military people returning to the civilian workforce, and underskilled or entry-level applicants including those from welfare-to-work programs—all people who may be lacking industry-specific results to measure. Motivation-Based Interviewing doesn't do this. It assesses the applicant's underlying attitude to determine consistency of achievement both in the long run and in varied circumstances.

Let me tell you more specifically why assessing results by themselves is flawed. First, if a person hasn't succeeded yet and has so far only failed but is still trying, you will shortchange this applicant because his record will lack results. Secondly, if a person has never had the opportunity to show what he can achieve but would relentlessly pursue great results once he had this opportunity, he currently has no results to measure either. This applicant would also be overlooked. And third, if the results happen to have come easily, you won't know whether you have a high performer or not. You won't know whether this applicant quits trying when the going gets tough.

You have to measure an applicant's ability to achieve results in the face of adversity—otherwise you cannot accurately predict future achievement. Low performers can produce results when there are no obstacles in their way. I don't think there is a job out there that doesn't encounter some kind of difficulty that needs to be overcome. You must evaluate how the applicant responds in the face of adversity. This is what separates the high achievers from those who are not.

To measure an applicant's ability to overcome adversity and conquer obstacles, you must look at how he thinks and responds to situations involving obstacles. Using the example in an earlier chapter, the telephone wasn't invented first and then thought of afterward. The thought of it being possible came first. Alexander Graham Bell had an idea and believed it could work. He focused on how to make it work, not on its lack of feasibility. He conceived it, believed it was possible, and then made it happen.

Not only does the thought have to come first, but it must be the right type of thought. It must be positive, focused on possibility and on how to attain it. There are people who don't think this way because they are unwilling to believe first. They want to see it first, and only then will they believe. They spend more time thinking and talking about why something isn't possible than why it is possible. They focus on the barriers in their way, on limitation, and on the negative aspects. Many of them give long dissertations explaining their viewpoints. When they do this, they are focusing on validating or proving impossibility. This keeps solutions from being uncovered.

Even though their mode of operation is to focus on the improbability, often they verbally express their desire for results. They expect results *without* having the right type of thoughts needed to produce the desired outcome. They think negative thoughts, yet wish for achieving positive results. What a contradiction! But we know that without the right thought, you don't expend the same effort to achieve the desired results. It's really not a mystery why some people achieve more results and others achieve much less.

MEANINGLESS WORDS
OR WORDS FULL OF MEANING?

In an interview, words about achieving results are truly meaningful only when they are backed by a mental attitude conducive to victory and then followed by effort. First of all, you must know that what an applicant says during an interview comes with no guarantee or warranty. Know that anyone can say anything. The fact that words are spoken doesn't make them absolute. Con-artists use smooth words but have nothing to back them up. They make their living by convincing people of something that isn't actually so. They have mastered the art of words. So have some applicants. I'm not suggesting that applicants are con-artists, not at all. But some of them manage to do a very good job convincing their interviewers that there is no one better to hire when, in fact, there is.

In an interview that lasts an hour or so, it's hard to get to know an applicant. Because of the relationship that exists between an interviewer and an applicant, some critical information may be inappropriate for an applicant to share during an interview. But that doesn't mean this information isn't possible to pick up on anyway. Often, if you take a look beyond the person's words, there are other clues present. These clues can offer great insight to an applicant's level of motivation and to her future performance but are often overlooked by untrained interviewers.

One of the best clues is not what an applicant says but what she does, her actions. The applicant's attitude that shows through during an interview can be a great tip-off for the interviewer because thoughts and actions are linked. And this connection is not dependent on any spoken words. Know that actions do not just randomly occur: They are governed by thought. An applicant's thought and attitudes cannot be concealed completely, even though some words may attempt to camouflage them.

Just as some words that are spoken are truly meant, others are only well intended. In an interview, words may be spoken only for the purpose of encouraging a job offer. It can be hard to tell the difference between the two (meaningful or meaningless words). When words are full of meaning, they are backed with matching action. There are no differences or contradictions between them. When words and actions correspond, this is referred to as being *congruent*. It means they are consistent with each other and are in harmony. They equal each other. What a person speaks of doing agrees with what she actually does. When an applicant talks of wanting an outcome and then does nothing, does something for only a short spurt, or does something completely different, this is *incongruent*. There is a discrepancy between the words and the behavior.

I remember this young woman I interviewed who told me that she really wanted the opportunity to be promoted from an hourly employee to a manager. She said she liked the company, wanted to stay, and was interested in moving up. It was a good conversation and I was aware that she did a good job as an hourly paid employee. As we talked further, I found out that she did not have her high school diploma or her GED. I told her this was a requirement for management, which it was. But I said we would seriously consider her if she met this requirement. Now the ball was in her court, and she needed to take action. Her words sounded gung-ho, but I never heard back from her. She talked about wanting to move into management but never followed through to make it happen. Getting her GED was an obstacle that she let stop her. Later, I heard she had lots of excuses for why she couldn't meet this requirement. And she said all of them happened to be out of her control. Her actions did not match her words.

But it's not always all action or none. Some people take some action and then stop. They do enough to get by only and do not advance from there. Instead of doing everything they can or everything that is necessary, they choose an easier road. They take action, but they take a shortcut, also known as the *path of least resistance*. It's a halfhearted, less committed attempt to reach the goal, but it doesn't involve ample action. Often it's just done for show. Especially in the case of career advancement, I have seen the path of least resistance taken many times, and never effectively. Here's an example:

During an interview, an applicant talks about wanting to get promoted and can't understand why he always gets passed up. He thinks it's not about his performance because he works hard. It's the system, he says. It's not fair. But let's take a look at his attitude and at the effort that he has expended to make himself the best choice for the promotion. Feeling that promotions are based on who you know and on favoritism, why should he break his back working hard when it won't make any difference? He considers his work good enough. He already knows that working harder won't make any difference. The problem isn't him; it's the boss and the company.

There is no connection between working hard and getting promoted. He thinks the boss doesn't understand the obstacles he encounters every day out there on the front line. Those people who were promoted instead of him didn't have it as tough as he did. In fact, they probably don't even know what tough is. They were basically lucky, and that's how they achieved their results.

About now he has had enough with this company. He decides it's time to find a new job. He believes it's his only option for getting promoted. It's never going to happen here.

He never inquires into what it will take to get promoted with this employer and never ends up expending the effort. Instead, he takes the path of least resistance and goes hunting for a new job. He takes this path of thinking because he doesn't make the connection between promotions and his efforts. He perceives having no control over this situation. During his interviews, this applicant talks about his successes, his desire for advancement and moving up the ladder, but also about why it will never happen with his current employer and he says it has nothing to do with him.

If you have been interviewing for any length of time, you've seen this scenario before, possibly many times. It's not the fact that he went job-hunting that's the issue or even that he didn't get promoted with his current employer; it's that he believes his actions are disconnected and unassociated with achieving his desired outcome, which is getting promoted. I believe that he genuinely wants the promotion but he perceives it to be someone else outside of himself who's responsible for his desired results. What I want to know is when did the applicant determine that getting promoted was impossible: Was it before or after he tried?

We know that achieving the goal doesn't come first in order to guarantee us it's going to happen at all. No one is provided with a warranty in advance that our effort will necessarily have the desired payoff. Unconditionally, the effort must come before any goal can be reached. But before the effort, the belief that results are indeed possible must come. First comes positive thought, then effort, then the goal—in that order.

When effort is expended, it always has the risk of not producing results on the first try or after boundless tries. This risk does not deter high performers from taking action, because inside they still believe they can and will achieve, one way or another. They have positive thought followed by positive action. Their words are made meaningful by the thoughts that precede them and the actions that follow them.

WHAT'S YOUR APPLICANT SAYING?

The O-SAE Method asks for information about how the applicant has handled past situations that involved obstacles. After the applicant provides some details regarding the situation, he will begin explaining what he did, specifically how he responded—the *A* portion of O-SAE. Here is where his perceived control or locus of control comes out. Read closely the information in this section.

Perceived control is the degree to which a person realizes that his actions and his lack of action are connected to and have an effect on an outcome. "I cans" and "I can'ts" come from a person's perceived control. When a person thinks he can, he perceives having control over the outcome. Conversely, when a person believes he cannot, he thinks he lacks the control to affect the outcome. Relinquishing control or disconnecting oneself from an outcome is what produces the words *I can't*. "I can't" is different from "I don't want to."

Whether an applicant connects with, or disconnects from, an outcome has a different effect on what comes next: his thinking about what to do or how to respond to obstacles. Those perceiving control, the "I can" people, think about what can be done to achieve results. These people can talk precisely about their decision for action and the reasoning behind it. It's only when an applicant has expended effort that he can talk in detail about the action he took.

On the other hand, when an applicant believes he lacks control, he isn't thinking about what action to take to reach the goal, because he thinks his actions won't have much of an impact. This applicant cannot talk in detail about the steps he takes to achieve results because he doesn't take these steps as often as someone who perceives more control. But what he can talk about easily is his reasoning for his lack of effort. In the face of adversity, applicants will express the belief either that they had some control to affect the situation or that they did not.

If the applicant believed he lacked control, then he must also believe someone else had it. Control is external of himself. The obstacle itself usually becomes his excuse for being unable to achieve the desired outcome. His inner voice, or his thought process, tells him that there is nothing he can do about it. He may desire to get around it but lacks the belief that he can. This is his particular perception of control, and that's what he talks about.

The clues start with the applicant's words. One of the easiest clues to listen for is the diverting of blame or the shedding of ownership. When control is relinquished, finger-pointing takes the place of accepting ownership ("There is nothing I can do about it, it's so-and-so's fault"). Commonly, phrases such as "It will *never* change" or "It will *always* be that way" are used to justify inevitable or hopeless doom. Explanations that shift control from oneself and onto someone or something else are a notable expression of an external perceived control. The focus is on what was external of themselves that had the control that prevented them from achieving desired results.

Remember, excuses and results have an inverse relationship. There is no need for both to be present at the same time. Excuses exist only as a substitute for results. The presence of an excuse means the absence of results and often the absence of effort. You'll find that when the applicant talks about his lack of control, he is *not* talking about the effort he has put in or of his results. Here are some sample expressions that show a belief in lack of control. These are usually followed by an explanation for why this thinking is justified.

External Clues (Lacking Control)

- I can't.
- It's impossible.
- It will never work.
- I have no control over it.
- It failed before and will fail again.
- It wasn't meant to be.
- It failed but wasn't my fault.
- It'll never change.
- It was never going to happen, so I had to give up.
- I can guarantee it won't work.
- I had no other choice.
- There was nothing I could do about it.
- Why bother? I already knew it wouldn't work.
- It's just bad luck.

Excuses come in all different shapes, sizes, and packages. They are one of the biggest indicators of thinking that lacks control. The magnitude or the quantity of obstacles that get in the way of results is not the issue, nor is the size of the obstacle the difference or a valid explanation for varying performance levels, contrary to what low performers think. Rather, the issue is the attitude toward moving past those things that are in the way. Moving past obstacles involves the active thought process of focusing on how it can be done, not on why it can't be done.

The Reverend Jesse Jackson said, "You many not be responsible for getting knocked down, but you're certainly responsible for getting back up." Those who don't get back up have quit, and quitting affects achievement. This is when excuses appear and are used to rationalize this halting of effort. Quitting is never marketed as just plain quitting. It's not socially acceptable, not in sports and not in the workplace—you're supposed to keep playing. And it especially doesn't sound good to say you quit trying during a job interview. Henceforth, the reason for quitting must be explained as being beyond one's own personal control. The applicant says he had no other option. For any excuse to work, it must sound legitimate and convincing.

You as an interviewer must not judge the merits or believability of the individual excuse but instead acknowledge excuses for what they really are.

WHAT'S YOUR APPLICANT REALLY DOING?

Excuses are a big clue but not the only clue, and they are not stand-alone clues. Actions tell "the rest of the story," to use radio commentator Paul Harvey's famous phrase. Actions or the lack of them are the additional clues needed to ascertain an applicant's locus of control. Actions are much more prevalent with those who are internally motivated than with those who are externally motivated. Measuring motivation requires quantifying expended effort. Here's another way of putting it: Under the pressure of hardship, how easily does an applicant quit expending effort and start making excuses? I want to know about the applicant's actions, specifically the effort he is expending in pursuit of the goal under these conditions.

When we are talking about overcoming obstacles and about reaching goals, in order for the words to be genuine, they must be followed by effort that is sustained long enough to achieve results. Spurts of effort just don't cut it. *Follow-through integrity* is the pattern of initiating action and persisting long enough to fulfill the promise of the words spoken. Simply put, it's the consistent habit of keeping one's word. It's putting in effort, not excuses, rationalization, or justification.

Take a moment and think about how the high performer and the low performer will talk about their perceived control to overcome obstacles that are in their way. Do you think they will sound exactly the same? Will each explanation involve the same amount of effort? If not, what do you think the distinctions will be? Can you recall from any past interviews some actual applicant responses where the quantity of effort or even the quantity of excuses varied? It's really not hard to see when you know specifically what you're seeking.

During an interview, three possible scenarios can exist regarding an applicant's words and the actions that will or won't follow:

Scenario 1

The applicant openly expresses his perception believing that he lacked control. He explains why there was nothing he could do to change the outcome and who or what was in control. When asked to talk about his effort, he's forced into revealing the lack of effort. Excuses become his explanation for his lack of action. What the applicant said and did somewhat align: Both the words and excuses imply no action and there was no action. The applicant's thoughts and words showed a lack of perceived control and were passive, and so were the applicant's actions. The actions that followed, if any, were insufficient to achieve results. If you do hire this person, don't expect a dramatic change in him, and don't expect a high performer.

Scenario 2

The applicant says all the right things. "Yes. Yes, I have the right attitude, I am positive!" He practically bursts out singing a few verses of "Everything is Beautiful." Okay, maybe the last part was an exaggeration, but you get my point. What the applicant has to say sounds great but happens to be all talk—a lot of hot air. This person has taken the advanced class on being interview-savvy. Guess what? When you ask for one example after another (using the O-SAE Method) for details on how he handled past obstacles, he can't provide specifics about his efforts. This is because he doesn't have any. The best he can do is give generic filler answers, the way we all handled essay questions in school when we didn't know the real answers. It was only when we knew, that we could provide precise information. As an interviewer, if you are unable to recognize this for what it is, "fluff," you won't get too far. You must ask for specific information and you must probe for more details if you don't automatically get them.

•••

These two scenarios have something in common: The words may have differed, but both lacked any detailed discussion of expended effort. It was the action—or, more specifically, the lack of it—that was more definitive than the words. Faced with having to determine which has more substance, words or actions, you should choose actions hands down. What an applicant does is a much better and more consistent indicator than his words.

Scenario 3

The applicant has the "Yes, yes, I can do it" attitude, says all the right things, and can, in fact, back up his words with specific and detailed accounts of where he displayed sustained effort. Here, the words and actions are consistent with each other. They are congruent. The words don't just have a positive spin; they are supported with substance. The applicant truly perceives control because his words are followed by action. Action validates or attaches meaning to words.

Even if this applicant lacks prior experience and skills in the field and cannot offer parallel industry examples, he can still talk about other past experiences that show he regularly expended effort. Having a history or strong pattern of applying effort toward conquering the obstacles already in place is a crucial component for all high performers.

•••

Out of the three scenarios just discussed, *all* of them have *equal* likelihood of happening in the future. The last one offers you as the interviewer the greatest potential for producing the most results, because this applicant is most likely to be a high performer. It's about assessing risk and placing your bet on the applicant with the greatest probability of success and the least chance of failure. To do that, you must ascertain predominant behavior.

HOW DO YOU KNOW
WHICH BEHAVIOR IS PREDOMINANT?

Are you okay hiring someone who can't quite achieve results regularly, as long as there's a good excuse for why? Have you noticed that it's almost as if some people are prevented from achieving results or cheated from success, yet there are others who aren't? Call it luck or call it whatever you like, I want to hire employees who will help move the company forward. Now we are getting down to the nitty-gritty.

We already discussed predominant behavior, also referred to as the blue-colored balls, which are the ones most likely to repeat. It's simple: If we want to be as accurate as possible at predicting someone's future job performance, then we must determine what behavior has occurred the most frequently in the past. This is the applicant information that we are going to use to project future performance and to make hiring decisions.

If you, as the interviewer, continuously request examples of an applicant's actions involving an obstacle using the O-SAE Method, a pattern of behavior will begin to emerge. The line of questions must be consistently formatted in order for a pattern to be seen. If you haphazardly ask questions or ask ones without obstacles, you're creating an interviewing environment in which a pattern may not become visible.

A pattern of behavior consists of more than one behavior. One excuse or one action is merely a clue, not a conclusion. It tells us nothing about how regular or how often a behavior occurs. An excuse by itself doesn't mean there is a rampant problem or that the applicant is externally motivated. Nor does a single action signify a high achiever.

You need to step back and take a look at the bigger picture in order to see which type of behavior occurs most often. And you must work with an entire interview of behavior information in order to see this bigger picture.

Assessing perceived control is not about looking for a single way of thinking within a person but rather looking for a way of thinking that is predominant. Both internal and external motivation ("I cans" and "I can'ts") exist within everyone. The truth is that everyone makes excuses, including myself. And it's not realistic to think there is a person out there who absolutely expends no effort ever or every effort always.

In every interview, with every applicant, you will hear some excuses and also some explicit examples of action. Assessing perceived control is discerning which is most prevalent. One of them actually dominates the thinking process—but which one? Finding the strongest pattern of behavior will tell us the answer.

ALGEBRA NOT REQUIRED

You should realize by now that we are looking for a specific pattern in how a person responds in the face of adversity. Responses to adversity in particular are filled with abundant locus of control information. When the applicant's path has been blocked with obstacles, first of all, what does she say? Then what does she do? We are looking for how she responds. Then from there, we are looking for a pattern of responses. There are only two different types of responses, not five, 10, or some mind-boggling number that will require that you to use algebra. We are looking for externally motivated responses, ones that lack perceived control, and internally motivated responses, where control is perceived.

ACTIONS VALIDATE WORDS

Applicants with perceived control—those who are internally motivated—will answer questions incorporating their optimistic "I can" attitude. If asked, they can provide a detailed description of their efforts. They have an attitude like The Little Blue Engine, the train in the children's book written by Wally Piper that said "I think I can, I think I can, I know I can, I know I can." And when the little engine made it over the mountain, it proclaimed, "I knew I could, I knew I could!" And those who have tried and those who have done it are the ones who can provide all the details about their effort. Count how many times you hear this type of answer. Listen for words and phrases that are positive and that are accepting of responsibility even if success hasn't happened yet. Here are the types of phrases to listen for:

Internal Clues (Perceived Control)

- I can and I did.
- I had to find a way to do it.
- I'm not going to give up.
- I'm sure it's possible.
- I'm still working on it!
- It can be done.
- We've got to think of creative solutions.
- I know I can make it work.
- I have obstacles, but I can overcome them.
- I will find a solution.
- Where there's a will, there's a way.
- There is an answer.

Don't count answers as clues to internal motivation unless, and only unless, they have matching effort and action accompanying them. Otherwise, they are empty words or merely good intentions. Believing in good intentions is a roll of the dice. They are words that are not represented with action. They suggest possible future action, but technically this makes them meaningless, because nothing validates them in the present. It is attached action that validates words. And action either will happen or it won't. The best bet for sizing up good intentions is to review the applicant's past pattern of making things happen or of following through. It is the consistent behavior that is most likely to repeat in the future, not the inconsistent behavior.

PROBLEM-FOCUSED

Another area for you as the interviewer to watch when you're looking for attached action is discovering *half-hearted* effort. On the surface it looks action-oriented, but underneath there is nothing of real substance. It is a façade that can trick interviewers or anyone else who wants to buy into it. Sometimes it's an external motivator that's causing the action and when this push or pressure subsides, so does the effort. It can be easily recognized for what it is, or more accurately what it isn't, if you just look for these things: Notice how *easily* or *quickly* an applicant abandons effort when an obstacle blocks his path, and notice what captures his focus. Is his focus primarily on the obstacles, the hardships, and the things that are wrong, broken, or bad? Is he focused on problems? Or is his focus on finding a way to get around these impediments and finding solutions? What is predominant?

Some people think their only option is to demand that someone else fix the problem or they will quit. They perceive that they'll have more of an influence by halting their effort than by participating in the solution. "Fixing" requires the thinking that your effort will have a payoff. In other words, it involves perceiving the control to make things happen. Those who don't try or who quit usually do not recognize their behavior as the problem or their thinking as the culprit.

Because of *The Interview Relationship,* applicants cannot admit to being people who can't find solutions or who give up easily. Watch out for the martyr or the "poor me" pitch attached to half-hearted effort. It markets the person being a real trouper who sadly had success stolen away by uncontrollable and unsolvable hardships. High performers, though, when faced with obstructions and setbacks, are likely to pick themselves back up and solve problems to achieve results—despite the roadblocks. The situation can be the same, but it's the attitude that differs. Be aware of convincing or sincere-sounding responses that lack genuine sustained effort.

1, 2, 3...Tallying Responses

Usually there will be a clear-cut line between a positive attitude and a negative one. Vocabulary heavy in words and phrases such as "I can't," "it will never work," "there's no way it can be done," and "there's nothing I could do about it" is negative and points to people who are externally motivated. These phrases customarily include blaming or shedding ownership to absolve oneself of responsibility of an outcome. This isn't present or necessary in explanations where control is perceived.

Some answers, however, are not so clear-cut. Don't worry about the applicant responses that seem inconclusive. For those that are not clearly one way or the other, or that you are unsure about, don't count them at all as a locus of control response. But for the ones that are apparent, *every* one of them must be counted, whether it's what you wanted to hear or not. Assessing locus of control is the tallying of all responses to adversity during an interview and determining which type of thinking, internal or external, is predominant. Know that not everything that is spoken will provide a locus of control clue.

Oftentimes motivation is viewed as something that either is or is not. It's a picture that depicts only one of two extremes with nothing in between. Is a person only 100-percent, fully gung-ho motivated or is he not motivated at all? Are those the only two choices we have? Is that how we have been assessing our applicants?

It's probably not realistic to classify our applicant's thinking in such extremes. He doesn't have to perceive total control over everything or absolutely no control over anything for you to be able to evaluate his locus of control. No one is 100-percent internally or 100-percent externally motivated. In reality, whether people are aware of it or not, their thoughts show a combination of internal and external motivation. Every applicant will provide a mixture of both positive and negative responses, of "I can's" and "I can'ts." Alongside a positive, action-oriented answer there will also be a negative, "that situation was out of my control" response. This is not unusual.

The Scale

Think of locus of control as a vertical scale that consists of internal motivation on the top of the scale and external motivation on the bottom. The scale is symbolic of the degree to which a person can motivate himself. At the top of the scale would be 10, which represents 100-percent internal motivation. At the bottom of the scale, zero represents the inability to self-motivate and the sole reliance on external factors to push or cause motivation, also known as external motivation.

Both a zero and a 10 on the locus of control scale are theoretical because no one is purely one or the other. Even a couch potato will get up off the couch to replace the batteries in his remote control, making him above a zero on the scale. My personal estimate is that most people in the United States fall somewhere between three and seven, a few points on either side of the midpoint of five.

A behavior pattern that *more often* shows an applicant as perceiving control and focused on possibility points to a person who is predominantly internally motivated. A pattern of behavior that *more*

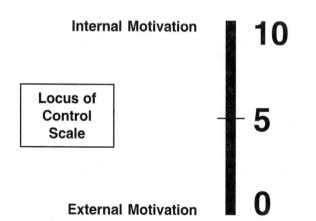

often reflects the abandonment of control and is focused on impossibility, limitations, and excuses shows the person is predominantly externally motivated.

It is the sum of all the information and not individual behaviors and responses that yields the answer to predominant behavior. An appreciable amount of applicant behavior should be examined and linked together to create a pattern of behavior or a bigger picture. Applicant responses should amass over the entire interview, from beginning to end. Rarely should one piece of information be used to make a hiring decision. The exceptions would include evidence of extreme inadmissible behavior, such as violence, theft, and other illegal behaviors.

Predominant "I can" attitude and "I did" behavior are considered above five on the scale. High performers are those people who *most often* embrace the power of positive thinking and then expend the effort to prove that their optimistic way of thinking is correct. It really is the same process that is going on with the low performer as it is with the high performer—proving your thought process to be right. The difference is that the high performer thinks he can and the low performer thinks he can't, and they both think they are right. The high performer proves that he is right by expending the effort and not quitting until he is right. And the low performer withholds action or dispenses it in limited supply to prove his thinking is right. Yes, it is true: Whether you think you can or cannot, you're right!

As an interviewer, you must determine on which side of the midpoint your applicant falls. Is it above the midpoint, with more perceived control responses, or is it below the midpoint, with more responses that show a perceived lack of control and only a few positive responses to adversity?

The numbers zero through 10 on the scale are not what is most important. The numbers are useful, but don't get too caught up in them. This is only an estimate, not a formal test. We are just adding a relevant piece information to the interview process to help us more accurately determine an applicant's future job performance. It's not actually a new piece of applicant information. It's existing information that we are learning to see in a new light and evaluate more precisely. It will help us better identify the high performers and also spot those applicants we should turn down.

Here is a good time to remind you to make sure the questions you ask do not lead the applicant to the "right" answer and that you aren't requesting only "happy-ending" answers. Those two mistakes will affect your results. This is also where listening becomes most important. Listening must be objective and bias-free or you, as the interviewer, could inadvertently focus on select responses or look to validate your own opinion. And if you don't listen closely, you increase your risk of incorrectly judging an applicant's predominant response to adversity and drawing the wrong conclusion.

There's No Such Thing as a Tie

When it comes to determining predominant behavior, I want you to realize something you cannot do. Let's say for the moment that you are assessing an applicant's skill level on a scale of one to five, with five being the highest or best rating. What would a three rating for a skill mean? It would denote "average" skill level, right? And it's correct to say that average would be an admissible rating.

Now, if the applicant provided an equal amount of internal and external responses, what would his predominant response be? Would it be "average"? Half-and-half denotes neither one as being predominant. It offers us no relevant information and therefore cannot be used.

A predominant response is required for assessing locus of control. If you happen to get stuck with an equal amount of each type of response, go into overtime until you break the tie. Simply continue asking for past behavior examples involving more obstacles. At some point you will have collected enough information to see one as being prevalent over the other.

Okay, ready to give it a try yourself? Read these interview questions and these actual applicant responses and see whether you can pick up on the locus of control response.

Q: Tell me about a time you discovered a problem with something and what you did to try to fix it before it became a bigger problem. What were the end results?

A: I discovered a problem with a security model that we were designing. To fix it, I changed one component from a view to a table, which allowed us to maintain referential integrity and that solved the problem.

Q: You told me you are job hunting because you believe your current company may be in financial trouble, because you are being asked to cut your budget by 10 percent. Tell me what you have done to try to reduce expenses and what the outcome was.

A: I've been managing this department for more than 10 years, and every year it takes more money to operate than the year before. I can't do a good job if the company always wants to cut back. There's just no way it can be done and that I can still do a good job.

Q: You talked about a project you were overseeing and said you were unable to complete it by the deadline date. What were the obstacles you and your team encountered, and how did you try to conquer them?

A: There were several weak links on the team who didn't complete key portions of the project on time. We had to wait until they were done first. They were busy and there was nothing we could do about that except just wait.

Well, the first response was internal and the second one was external—there was one of each. It's the last one that swings us to a predominant response. That last response was also external. We counted one internal response and two external responses, making the greater quantity of responses ones that show a belief in a lack of control or evidence of external motivation. Now, this was only a mini-exercise and a small sampling of applicant responses, which wouldn't really be enough to use to accurately deduce an applicant's locus of control. In most interviews that last an hour or so and use the O-SAE Method of formatting interview questions, you will reap roughly a dozen usable examples of responses to adversity.

The More He or She Truly Believes

Now that you have a fair amount of behavioral responses to work with, the zero-through-10 numbers on the locus of control scale come in handy. Let me explain this by using a cat's behavior as an example of perceived control affecting motivation. When the cat becomes hungry and wants to be fed, he expends effort pestering his owner for food. The cat, to some degree, believes his effort will eventually pay off with food, his desired outcome. The more the cat believes his efforts will produce the desired results, the more relentlessly he pesters his owner. And the less he believes his efforts will pay off, the less he will persist, if he even bothers to try at all.

We want to look at the degree to which a person believes he can or cannot achieve desired results. This will help us determine how persistent the applicant will be. The less mixed an applicant's responses are between internal and external—or maybe a better way to put it, the more the answers are of one type—the stronger he believes whatever it is he believes, either that he can or he can't. The more he believes he can achieve, the more outright persistent he will be. And the more he believes that he can't achieve results, the less effort he will put into trying.

Using the numbers on the scale is a good way to reference the variance between applicants. This is also useful for referencing the quantity or degree of perceived control or the lack of it. To what degree will an applicant expend the effort in order to makes things happen? Is it a lot of effort or just a little? Is the applicant extremely internally motivated or only slightly? Perhaps he is extremely externally motivated or maybe just a bit.

The degree to which an applicant is internally or externally motivated does not need to be a precise measurement. If an applicant provides 10 locus of control clues, six of which are internally motivated answers and four of which are external clues, this applicant is slightly more internally motivated. If he gives us nine internal clues and only one external response, his attitude toward conquering obstacles and achieving results is very strong.

At this point, you really don't need me to tell you what to do here. Decide for yourself. Start putting this piece to work. It's not the interviewer's decision-making process that has been broken; that works just fine. It's the applicant information that's being used to make the hiring decision that's been the cause of bad hiring choices.

Continue to place your bet on the applicant you think will most likely achieve results. Now, what's different is you have more information—and it's not just any information: It's specific information that is relevant for predicting future performance. You decide who is the best hire, the applicant with the strongest pattern of overcoming obstacles or the interview-savvy applicant who talks about success but ends up exposing more excuses than effort. It really isn't rocket science.

ONE LAST NOTE:
THE INTERVIEWER'S LOCUS OF CONTROL

The more someone is externally motivated, the more he will use excuses. This applies to everyone, including interviewers. The more externally motivated the person conducting the interview is, the more he will be sympathetic to an applicant's excuses.

The more you use excuses, the more you accept them from other people and buy into them as being an acceptable reason for a lack of action. The interviewer's own locus of control can haze his or her view of the applicant and damage objectivity. It is unrealistic to think that every interviewer possesses a high internal locus of control.

In my experience, most people have a tendency to self-evaluate their own locus of control on the high side. I think that's customary, but it is important to understand how that affects applicant assessment and hiring. Make sure you have the right people in the job of employee selection.

Chapter 10

Assessing the Selfish Boss

Many applicants who lack a high level of interest in a job are hired and then coerced into accepting the company's goals as their own. There is somewhat of an expectation that all new hires are highly motivated. Managers are actually surprised when they discover that many of their employees are not very motivated at all. They don't understand why so many employees appear to be indifferent about the very jobs they were hired to do. Then these managers use performance evaluations, counseling, rewards, and incentives to compensate for what they didn't hire in the first place. Instead, we should take a look at the role we played in hiring employees who were indifferent toward doing their jobs.

Bad Person or Bad Occupation?

What is a bad hire, anyway? Is it a bad person? Are we talking about the employee's quality of character? Do we mean that the person is either good or bad? No. When we're talking about a good or a bad hire, we are talking about the degree to which an employee performs his job. It's performance that we are classifying as being good or bad.

Could it be that a bad hire is really a good person but is someone who has made a not-so-good career choice? That it's his occupation that is the issue and not the person? That perhaps the employee is not really "bad," he is just in the wrong job? And that in the right job this employee would have been a "good" hire?

Every human being, without exception, has the potential to reach great personal heights. The most crucial part of personal achievement, and the most difficult part for some people, is figuring out what it is they really want to be doing. Just because an applicant doesn't know this about himself yet, that does not have to stop employers in the quest to hire high performers.

Many years ago I conducted an exit interview on a retail manager. The company had decided to demote the struggling manager back into an hourly position just a little more than a year after promoting him. The company had spent the past six months working with him in an attempt to improve his job performance, but the effort was unsuccessful. Instead of being demoted, this manager (I'll call him Mike, but that's not his real name) chose to leave the company for another job. Mike had accepted a new job as a manager at a video store.

During the exit interview, Mike confessed that what he really wanted to do was pursue a career in computers. According to his supervisor, Mike's performance suffered in the areas of employee and customer relations. Mike himself expressed his own personal frustration in dealing with both of those areas. He really disliked the constant requests for special days off from the employees, and he especially disliked dealing with any customer who had a complaint.

Not surprisingly, Mike spent most of his time behind the scenes in the back of the store, away from people, doing inventory, and working on a computer program to support a marketing mailer he had developed in taking initiative on a task that was not part of his job. Naturally, he gravitated toward what he enjoyed doing and avoided those areas he disliked. Mike was not a *bad* person, nor was he lazy. On the contrary, there was a reason he was promoted into management in the first place. He was a conscientious employee.

This particular job, however, required that Mike do mostly tasks he disliked and only a few he liked. Just like anyone else, he took the most initiative in those areas that interested *him* the most. Unfortunately, Mike's area of interest was different from what the company was most interested in having him do. The problem wasn't that Mike was a bad person; it was that the job wasn't right for him or he wasn't right for the job, depending on how you look at it. The job as a retail manager wasn't a good match with Mike's interests, strengths, or goals.

Mike chose to continue his career in retail management at the video store because he lacked the education or experience needed to get hired right away as a computer programmer. And I am sure the person who interviewed and hired him at this video store did so because of his past management experience. This interviewer was correct in his thinking that Mike could do the job. But a job change to another company where he would do similar work would not fix the problem Mike was having with his job performance. The majority of the responsibilities in his new job would require him to do those same things he disliked doing the most: dealing with customer and employee issues.

This all had started over a year earlier with a friend of Mike's telling him about a job opening where he worked. His friend highly recommended both the company and the job to him and also recommended Mike to his manager, who was hiring. Mike was interviewed and hired almost on the spot, and that's how he got his start in the retail industry. Now Mike has experience in this industry to put on his resume, allowing him to more easily move into other retail jobs.

That's not where the story ends. Mike kept in touch with me for a while. After working at the video store for about six months, he figured out for himself that he was in the wrong type of work. He found a way to go back to school to get his degree in computer science, which was what he really wanted to be doing the most! The last time I spoke with him, he said he was doing great. He was no longer working at the video store and had landed a job as a programmer. He discovered that he was able to easily excel at it and was enjoying it tremendously.

It's not peculiar that Mike's job performance issues also paralleled exactly with his likes and dislikes. He had learned the necessary skills to do his job, but this job consisted mainly of tasks that were contrary to his interests. Nobody's motivation level is intensified by performing tasks that don't interest them.

Applicants may have the right attitude to achieve and even the right skill set to do the job, but if they are lacking a *bona fide* interest in it, their performance won't be equal to that of a high performer. A high level of interest is what accentuates motivation. To reach the performance level that a high performer does, there must be a match between the applicant and his job.

CAREER FIT

Yes, high performers love their work. They are personally interested in it—they want to be doing it. It is their interest that internally motivates them. This interest is also what bonds or connects them to the work. This connection is the reason so much energy is put into doing it. Because it's interest that causes motivation, then a job filled with a person's interests will bring about the highest level of motivation. It stands to reason, then, that the greater the applicant's interest in a job, the greater his potential for high performance.

The high performer's interests and his job mirror each other. Hiring must complement this, not ignore it. The applicant's interests, day-to-day job duties, and responsibilities need to be very compatible. They need to be one and the same or at least very close. If you remember from an Chapter 8, this is called *career fit*. When matching interests are accompanied by a "can-do" attitude, high performance emerges. This is a win-win because everyone's goals, both the company's and the employee's, are achieved.

PLUGGING IN

Let me go one step further and provide an analogy that will help you to better understand this relationship. It is critical that you comprehend this 100 percent. Think of a person laden with passion or motivation who wants to be, let's say, a computer programmer, like Mike. Think of this person as the plug on the end of an electrical cord. He is ready and able to transfer energy, but in order for electricity to flow, he needs a site to dispense his aptness. He needs a place to plug into. The applicant is the plug and the job is the electrical outlet. Not every plug will fit every outlet. There is more than one type of each. A receptacle can be 110 or 220 volts, it can be grounded or not, and it can be polarized or not. It can be a three-phase outlet, 12 volt DC, 50, or 60 Hz—get the point?

Picture a job as being an outlet that allows bottled-up energy or motivation to be unleashed and to flow. For the most energy to flow, there must be a good electrical connection. The plug and the outlet must match. I remember having a clothes dryer with one type of plug and an outlet of a different type. I had to have one of them changed in order for the dryer to work.

Here's an example: For the person whose greatest interest is programming computers, the best outlet would be a job where he could do computer programming. The similarities between the applicant's interests and the job are identical, thus allowing the greatest motivation or current to flow. You should know that this current doesn't flow in just one direction. It flows back to the employee in the form of personal satisfaction and fulfillment that comes from doing what he loves. This connection has a natural way of reducing turnover.

The connection is crucial for the best energy transfer to happen. Simply put, the connection really refers to how much similar interest the two share. A sales position and a computer programmer are different and would not have the same connection or the same flow of voltage. High performers have simply plugged into a matching outlet.

As a reminder, we know it's unrealistic to expect employees to change who they are to fit the job. The better strategy is to hire the right match, someone who has *bona fide* interest in the job. I want to say this enough so it really sinks in. The trouble that most interviewers have with this portion of assessment is that they want it to be more black and white to them, or less gray. Usually we have no trouble associating the lack of skills with the lack of performance, but we sometimes have difficulty believing that the lack of interest is connected to poor performance.

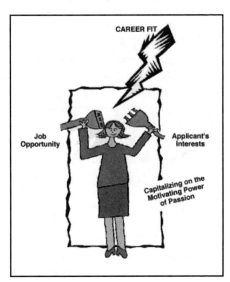

Unlike skills, however, low interest does

not necessarily mean that the applicant will be unable to perform the job as he would if he lacked the skills. Because of this difference between interest and skills, skills are often given higher ranking in applicant selection. This notion is merely an illusion. Just as performance suffers when an employee lacks the know-how to do a job, performance is also affected when the job does not match the applicant's interests. How well a person performs his job is directly connected to his interest in doing that job. You need to start believing it if you don't already.

We know that skill development is ongoing. Skills can be forgotten, taught to someone, even improved upon. Interests are not so amenable. It's interest that feeds motivation, whereas skills lack any authority to influence it. If skills were motivators, this book would be about how to hire the highly skilled—but it's not. Because the focus is on how to hire high performers, an applicant's interests cannot be ignored. Without uncovering and evaluating an applicant's interests and comparing them to the job, hiring high achievers becomes merely luck.

THIS IS NOT NEW— YOU'RE ALREADY DOING IT

Evaluating a match between an applicant's interests and the job is not as foreign as you may think. You are currently doing something very similar in your interview process now. Interviewers gather information about the applicant's skills by asking some related questions in order to determine level of skill. Then this skill information is compared with the duties and responsibilities of the job. The closest match is usually hired, right?

Assessing interests is done exactly the same way. The *only* variation is that you are comparing the applicant's interests with the job instead comparing skills with the job. It's the same comparison using different applicant information. You are using those five specific questions to gather this information. And because you already know enough about the job to be able to compare the applicant's skills with it, you'll have no problem also comparing the applicant's interests to the job. With skills, you are assessing whether the applicant *is able* to do the job. With interests, you are assessing whether he *wants* to do it or is motivated to do it. That's the difference. And you'll need to do both, not just one or the other.

Now, do you remember those five questions used to assess interest level? Well, it's okay if you don't yet. Before you know it you'll be asking them to every applicant out of habit. Let's bring them back now.

1.   Out of the jobs you've had, which was your favorite? Why?

2.   Which one was your least favorite? Why?

3.   On your last performance evaluation, in which three areas were you rated the highest?

4.   On your last performance evaluation, tell me the two areas in which you received the lowest rating and needed improvement.

5.   Tell me about your career goals for the next two to five years.

Obtaining information about interests involves asking each applicant these questions pertaining to *likes, dislikes, strengths, weaknesses,* and *goals.* You are welcome to create and ask more than these five provided. Answers will fall into one of two groups. The first group will consist of applicant answers that reference *likes, strengths,* and *goals.* These are questions one, three, and five. The second group will consist of the applicant's *dislikes* and *weaknesses.* This information will come from questions two and four. Both groups of questions, however, are really used to frame the applicant's interests.

Likes and *goals* are the strongest of the indicators that reflect an applicant's interests. And because most people are better at doing the things they like than they are at doing the things they dislike, an applicant's *strengths* are important barometers also. It's easy to get this particular information because most people like talking about their special aptness. It's a topic they know well. You can even ask children and watch them light up when they talk about what they can do well. People never lose this.

Conversely, *weaknesses* usually reflect a person's *dislikes.* The exception is when someone states that he has great interest in pursuing and developing a particular area in which he has had no opportunity as of yet. Timing-wise, or for the moment only, it's a weakness. For those who have had plenty of opportunity and haven't developed the skill into a strength, it's likely that particular area is not of primary interest to them. For example, you don't see me chasing any opportunity to learn more about accounting. It's not my strength or my interest. I know enough to get by, just as I do with expense reports. Procrastination or the lack of action occurs foremost with those tasks that are least favored.

A word of warning needs to be attached here. For people who have had opportunity and have not made the most of it, realize that admitting this may be inappropriate during an interview. To make sure the applicant's statement is not empty and without meaning, you need to see effort attached in pursuit of this goal to substantiate it as being genuine. They may say they had great intentions but didn't have the time or make some other excuse for not following through.

You may be asking only three questions related to likes and two questions related to dislikes, but you'll also be gathering information from other questions throughout the interview. For example, the reason an applicant left a job will tell you about what he doesn't like. And the reason he accepted a new job will provide information about what he likes and what's important to him.

The questions about the past performance evaluation are not going to provide the only strength and weakness information in the interview. You'll find out more when you're assessing the applicant's skills. Some applicants are very candid about the parts of the job they loved as well as the parts they didn't. All of this information will help you build a picture of what motivates a person and can be used to compare and determine whether the job you're trying to fill would be a good fit.

No Right or Wrong Answers

There is no score sheet to check an applicant's answers that will instantly tell you whether his interests match the job. That's too bad, because you could just grade the answers and be done with this assessment. But if evaluating a match were that absolute, applicants would quickly learn the "right" answers to give.

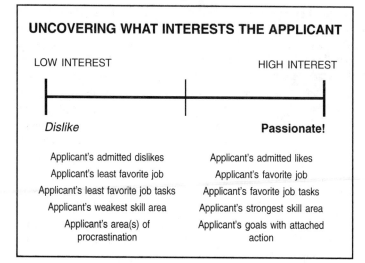

UNCOVERING WHAT INTERESTS THE APPLICANT

LOW INTEREST   HIGH INTEREST

Dislike   **Passionate!**

Applicant's admitted dislikes	Applicant's admitted likes
Applicant's least favorite job	Applicant's favorite job
Applicant's least favorite job tasks	Applicant's favorite job tasks
Applicant's weakest skill area	Applicant's strongest skill area
Applicant's area(s) of procrastination	Applicant's goals with attached action

This part of applicant assessment allows you not only to assess seemingly qualified candidates but also to include applicants you otherwise would not include, and that's particularly great in an industry that is starving for applicants. You can see that if an applicant has weak or missing skills, if he is underqualified at the time of your job opening, he could still be a potentially great hire—a future high performer—with just a little training. Rather than instantly ruling out these candidates, you can switch your focus from skill assessment to interest assessment. Skills aside, you want to know how motivated the applicant is to do this job. You may discover that you have a highly motivated applicant just waiting for an employer to invest in him. This scenario could actually have better results than if you hired someone already skilled but with less interest or less motivation to do the job.

There are an infinite number of differences between jobs when you think about it, and therefore there really are potentially an infinite number of "right" and "wrong" answers applicants could provide. Assessing interest level is merely a process of matching similarities. A match or a mismatch between an applicant and a job hinges on the interests of one particular applicant and the day-to-day duties of one particular job. Because it is a comparison with one specific applicant to one specific job only, there are no absolute right or wrong answers that will apply to all jobs or to every applicant.

For example, when I was assisting with an interview awhile back, an applicant expressed that his least favorite part of his current job was working on Web page design. He didn't like doing that part of his job very much. Is this a good or a bad answer? Hopefully you figured out that it is neither right nor wrong in itself. For this information to be of use, it needs to be applied to a specific scenario. Once it is, then it takes on meaning, but not before.

It just so happened that this applicant was interviewing for a job that was about 95 percent Web page design. So how much of a match is there between this applicant and this job? Now that you know what the job is and have a basis for comparison, the information takes on meaning.

I know right about now you're asking, "What applicant would shoot himself in the foot by saying that?" It's a great question. You are becoming fully aware of the impact *The Interview Relationship* has on hiring. This applicant was screened prior to the interview and was found to have the necessary qualifications to do this job. He had prior information systems experience along with the skills to write applications and design Web sites. His resume looked satisfactory for the job, and he had enough knowledge and skills to talk about what he had done and was able to do. The applicant had good communication skills and interviewed well to this point.

For this particular job, designing a Web site was only a temporary project, but it was going to be a big portion of the job for the next year or so. When the project was finished, the job would revert back to include many other responsibilities, ones this applicant actually would like doing. This one-year project, however, was very important. It would have tight deadlines and a lot of work. The applicant selected would need to be self-motivated and would have to hit the ground running— with no excuses.

I wasn't the one conducting this interview, but the interviewer was very smart. He knew he shouldn't provide too much information about the job opening early on in the interview. Interview-savvy applicants can customize their answers to fit what they think the interviewer wants to hear if they get the information needed to do this. It's essential to provide applicants with information about the job, but there are better times and places than at the start of an interview. Simply holding specific job details until the end of the interview benefits the interviewer.

This interviewer asked the applicant about his likes and dislikes, his strengths and weaknesses on his last evaluation, and his career goals. Lo and behold, the applicant shared. But do you think applicants would share personal information about themselves that would purposely damage their chances of a job offer? Absolutely not!

Fake or altered answers offer no benefit to you as the interviewer. An honest answer may not be the answer you wanted to hear, but it is instrumental in helping you make good hiring decisions. Mismatched applicants who alter their answers to fit the job could easily be mistaken as good hires with adequate skills. But once they're employed, their work level will be much below that of a high performer.

Because Web page design was so important and was also 95 percent of this job for the next year or more, it was fairly easy to conclude that a match did not exist between this applicant and this job. However, some of you might be stuck in your old habit of hiring and might be saying, "Well, as long as he could do the job, so what about the other stuff?" Here I would encourage you to reconsider your position, because you are ignoring the impact interest level has on job performance.

Introverts and Extroverts

You'll notice that likes and dislikes are often a reflection of person's natural personality type. For example, people who are extroverted, or outgoing, favor jobs that give them a chance to interact with people. In fact, you'll often find that their best skill or strength is in dealing with people, such as providing top-notch customer service or resolving people-related problems. Their weaknesses are often in the opposite areas, such as the non-people tasks of doing paperwork or using computers.

Introverts are just the opposite. They are most comfortable working with "things," such as working on a project or crunching numbers. Don't get me wrong: It's not that introverts can't work with people; it's that they usually prefer jobs that allow them to focus more on objects or tasks and less on people. Mike the retail manager was a good example of an introvert.

Extroverts reenergize themselves just by being around people. Introverts require less social interaction and reenergize by being alone. Introverts need "down time" away from people to recharge their batteries.

Without even knowing me personally, can you figure out which personality type I am? The clues you have so far are that I am a public speaker and trainer and my passions are interviewing and hiring. You also know that I hate doing expense reports. Yes, I am an extrovert, very much so. I never get tired of being around people. Because I'm on the go a lot, sometimes I feel tired when I start speaking to a group, but it doesn't take me more than a few minutes to fully re-charge myself.

Being one or the other personality type is not better or worse, good or bad. It's just a matter of personal preference. Everyone has their own attributes and their own contributions to make in an indi-vidual way. When we label one type as either good or bad, it's because we are comparing it to requirements for a job. If the personality type accentuates performance, then it is good. But if it clashes with or hurts performance, it is, of course, considered bad.

We often try to modify the person to fit the job instead hiring well. We beat up and blame the individual for what we didn't do right in the first place. Saying that one personality type is bad or that one is better is nonsense, and so is trying to change a person to fit a job.

Is It a Match or a Mismatch?

Every job is made up of a combination of tasks. The tasks them-selves are neither enjoyable nor distasteful. What makes them one way or the other is how an employee feels about doing them. Be careful not to prelabel a task as being good or bad, likeable or not. Unless you will be the one doing this task, instead of hiring someone to do it, don't cloud it with your irrelevant opinion.

A job match is solely dependent on how much interest the applicant possesses in it. A job would not be much of a match for a particular applicant if it consisted mostly of tasks he found tedious, tasks he dis-liked, or tasks that brought him very little enjoyment for whatever reason. A task that one person finds enjoyable is not a task everyone necessarily enjoys. Because it is an individual preference, all applicants must be fully evaluated for their own interests.

Once I came very close to having that perfect job match *for me*. I was responsible for overhauling a company's hiring process. I had a great assistant, Connie, who would do my expense reports. For me, this job consisted of doing 99.9 percent of the things I personally loved to do. I could eat, drink, and sleep this job and work at it almost around the clock, I was so motivated to do it. On the norm, however, most jobs include more of a medley of a person's likes and interests, along with his least favorite and not-so-good-at tasks. Interest assessment simply involves the process of evaluating this match/mismatch combination.

A Package Deal

I was in a grocery store one day, standing at the bakery department counter waiting to be helped. Straight in front of me about 10 feet away was the employee working in that department. I was the only customer there but had to wait about five minutes before she ever acknowledged me. She was focused on packaging fresh-baked muffins and never bothered to look up. Instead of being customer-focused, the most important trait in a retail job, she gravitated to what she enjoyed more: a task not involving people. Whenever I feel "invisible" as a customer, the first thing I think is, *Who hired this person to do this job?*

Let me take a moment and say that I believe the number-one problem plaguing the customer-service industry is that the wrong people are hired to do customer-service jobs. When we talk about a compatible match between the person and the job, someone who shies away from people interaction is not an ideal hire for a job requiring a lot of people contact.

What a difference it makes having the right person in the right job. Customer service also offers many great examples of hiring done right. The great customer service experiences I've personally had and the best stories I've been told always have involved employees who chose to go the extra mile. And those employees providing that great service are merely gravitating to what they like doing, but this time it's compatible with their job. Customer service is not just about having a great policy in place or simply about training the people you do hire. It is a package deal that starts with selecting the right employees.

An employee who is in the wrong job or profession is like a fish out of water—not a good match, especially for the fish. If you are going to hire a fish, put him in a job with water, where he can swim and do what fish do well, a job that complements his natural abilities instead of clashing with them. And if you choose to hire a fish, let him be a fish. Don't expect or require him to be something else, to like something he doesn't, or to perform well out of water. Only in his natural environment is it possible for the fish to be fully energized and highly motivated. And out of water he will never be a high performer; he will only flounder, and that's the moral of this story.

LIKED MORE THAN DISLIKED

Comparing a job and an applicant to each other requires us to talk about the degree of a match or a mismatch. On the interest level scale, let's place the numbers zero through 10. To the far right on the scale there is "passion," which is 10. To the far left is "dislike," and it's zero. This makes sense because dislike is a total lack of interest, or zero interest. When an applicant neither likes nor dislikes a job, that is "indifference," or the midpoint on the scale falling halfway between passion and dislike.

Because "indifference" is neutral, having no strong appeal or displeasure, a job match can exist only above the midpoint. If there are an equal number of tasks that are of interest or are liked as tasks that are disliked or of no interest, then the job isn't one that will be liked more than it will be disliked. It's 50-50. The job must be liked more than it is disliked for there to be a good match.

When you assess locus of control, you are looking for one of two outcomes: predominant internal or external motivation. Similarly, when you assess an applicant's interest level in doing a job, you are looking for one of two outcomes, not 10. All you really need to know is whether there is predominantly a match between the applicant and the job or whether there isn't.

Just as when you're assessing locus of control, you should realize that no one answer would provide you with a conclusion. You will need to step back and spend the entire interview listening for and gathering applicant information. Anytime you want to determine anything that is most *predominant*, you must look at the big picture and not focus on the details.

When we refer to a predominant match regarding interests, the applicant must have *many* of his interests correspond to the day-today job duties. The job must be comprised more of an applicant's likes, strengths, and goals than of anything else. This is what makes a predominant match and one where motivation is unleashed into the job. It is in this scenario that job performance has the backing of the all-powerful motivating influence of interest. In order to tap into and use this power, there must be at very minimum a 51-percent match between the applicant's interests and the job—a predominant match.

The numbers on the scale are used to symbolize the degree—or, to be more exact, the percentage—of how much an applicant's likes or interests do match the job. Eighty percent is a very good match. It refers to approximately an 80-percent match between the job and what the applicant likes and wants to do, with only about 20 percent of his dislikes and weaknesses being part of the job. The job where I had that great assistant was almost a 100-percent match for me. It perfectly complemented my strengths, my highest interests, and my professional goals at the time. It also did not require me to achieve in those areas of my weakness or lack of interest. It so happened that the job and my passion were truly one and the same. I was so gung-ho to do that job, I was willing to do whatever it took to do great work. I even chose to sacrifice some of my personal life to spend more time doing exactly what I loved to do, and it was very satisfying.

When I look back at each job I've had in the past, I can see a direct parallel between my interest level in that job and my motivation level to do it. I remember this one particular job that I stayed in for only a very short time. It was a terrible match for me, because it was comprised of tasks I hated doing. This job actually was more of a match with my dislikes. It probably consisted of 20 percent or less of those things I liked to do. I didn't enjoy the work, none of my goals were being met there, and I wasn't very motivated to do that job. It's funny, because I can remember how long the day seemed. I couldn't wait for the end of each day to arrive, and I couldn't wait until I got another job so I could quit. I wish I had known then what I know now. I would have known better than to accept that job.

Added Dimension

You realize that the interest level assessment is only an estimate, not a formal test. But it is a very useful tool for gauging motivation. In most cases, the skill-assessment rating is also only an estimate that is somewhat arbitrarily assigned by the interviewer. The fact that they are estimates does not negate the usefulness or effectiveness of skill assessment and interest-level assessment. They're just pieces of information that will aid you as the interviewer in making a good hiring decision.

The more the applicant is interested in the job, the more he will enjoy doing it and the more he will be motivated to do it. None of us gravitates toward or wishes for more of our dislikes to be incorporated into our job. We have more than enough of those already, and adding tasks that are uninteresting to us certainly would not be a way to increase our level of motivation or output. I keep telling you that this is not rocket science. It's easy to comprehend, it is common sense, and it is not difficult to incorporate into your employee selection process.

Let me give you one more piece of insight here. You've heard of the saying, "The only constant is change." Realize that jobs are also something that are constantly undergoing change. Try to anticipate any upcoming changes or shifts in responsibilities and incorporate these into your assessments of both interests and skills. What currently is a 60-percent job match may only be a 40-percent job match six months down the road, which will have a negative effect on motivation. I always recommend an estimated 70-percent to 80-percent match between the applicant and the job whenever possible. Not only is this a strong predominant match having a positive effect on motivation, but it also allows room for change without having a dramatic negative impact.

The benefit in assessing the applicant's interest in doing a job has been known for a long time. Even if you are being introduced to this for the very first time, realize that it has already been determined to be useful. All we are doing is learning how to apply it or use it better. This information will help you identify the high performers and weed out those applicants who are only pretending to be. As you begin to gather this applicant information and incorporate it into your decision-making process, you will see how easy it is to use and the added dimension it offers. Now it is time to pull all of this information together.

CHAPTER 11

TO HIRE OR NOT TO HIRE—
THAT IS THE QUESTION

N ow that you realize the power that passion possesses, what exactly it consists of, and that its assessment is simply a comparison or matching process, it's time to combine it with locus of control. *Motivation* or motive in motion, when examined closely, is just a combination of a person's interests along with his perceived control. This is what ultimately determines motivation. Whether we are talking about an applicant, you, or me, the same principle is at work and it applies universally.

All along we have been talking about the components that personally connect someone to an outcome or results. The difference between locus of control and interest is that one is the connection between a person's action and the effect it is believed to have on an outcome and the other is the emotional connection. This is what personally connects someone to the outcome so that he cares one way or another about what happens. Positive thought or "buy-in" must come first. This prerequisite is required to command the personal action or initiate the effort that will potentially affect the outcome. After all, the lack of effort or a "why bother" attitude will never sway an outcome in the same way as the contribution of effort.

HIRE THE MOTIVATION—TEACH THE SKILL

You have learned about two very powerful components of motivation. Neither one can effectively work alone to produce a high level of motivation. Locus of control is the program running in a person's head that determines attainability with either an "I can" or "I can't" perception, but it is not the mastermind. It's the motion-mind. Still there needs to be an interest. Locus of control is like gasoline, a fuel that is dormant until it is mixed with a spark. It needs this spark to ignite it and to keep it burning. It's the spark that converts this dormant fuel into a useable energy that produces motion and results. And that spark is interest. The gasoline and the spark are as essential part of motivation, and both components must be taken into consideration when you are selecting employees. In the past, we have traditionally based our decisions on skills alone and we have gotten very mixed results. That should have told us awhile ago that there was something else, some other factor or factors that we were still missing. But they are missing no longer.

After reading this book to this point, let's say that you are humming along through the interview and you are now able to pick up on the applicant's locus of control. You can hear the clues and now know how to get the rest of the information. You want to learn whether action and effort are attached or whether action-less excuses are offered up instead. You also now realize you should add up all this information to see which behavior is most predominant, the "I can" attitude or one that more often says "I can't" or "it can't be done." You're doing great, and it's easier than you thought it would be! You are starting to pick up on the applicant's attitude to achieve or, in many cases, his lack of it.

Using the O-SAE Method allows you to gather both locus of control and skill information at the same time. However, these two assessments differ because one requires that you evaluate individual answers and the other requires you to examine an accumulation of answers to determine a predominant response. I assume that you know which one pertains to skill assessment and which one to locus of control, right?

Because locus of control information is gathered through skill-assessment questions, all you really have to do is make sure your questions are phrased well so that they are as effective as they possibly can be. This usually requires that you tweak what you have already been using. When it really comes down to it, all you are really adding to your interview process are five questions that will indirectly tell you about an applicant's interests. Nothing is being taken away. It really will have a tremendous impact on improving your selection of employees, and it's not even complicated.

Along with comparing an applicant's skills to the job to determine whether he can do it, you are also now comparing how much his interests match with the duties of the job. This is the information you gain from those five additional questions. With this you can determine whether the job duties and the applicant's interests are more of a match or whether the job consists mostly of tasks that don't interest the applicant. Which one is predominant? We can no longer be naïve about how this natural motivator works or ignore the impact it has on job performance.

Let's recap the applicant information that you have gathered so far. You have a good idea of the skills he possesses and the level to which they are developed. You also have evaluated the applicant's predominant responses to determine whether he is externally motivated, making excuses and shedding ownership for lack of results, or internally motivated, with a positive outlook and a solid pattern of finding solutions and expending effort without quitting. In addition, you have determined whether there is a parallel or a match between the job's duties and responsibilities and the applicant's likes and interests.

Okay, you may be willing to say you are following this so far, but you also have to admit you don't quite know what to do with all this information yet. We have indeed shed a new light on motivation. Now we must incorporate this information into making our hiring decisions.

In the past, you probably felt that a perfect skill match was an absolute must for the job. But now, hopefully, you are realizing that perhaps what is more important is to hire someone who is highly motivated to do the job even if he is lacking in skills. In a somewhat limited pool of applicants, this may be at times as close as you can get to hiring a high performer, that is by hiring the motivation and teaching the skill. I'm not suggesting that this is a viable option for every job, but it is time you start considering it. Because skills are the part of this formula that can be added or changed after the hire and the other components cannot, let's take skills out of the picture for the moment. The reason we do this is because if the applicant is lacking in any one of these areas and you are forced to compromise, in many cases, skills is usually the best place.

Before you or any other interviewer can think about making a hiring decision that involves compromising on skills, you must first consider whether you have the means, mode, and opportunity to train an employee once he is hired. Essentially what's being said here is that you must have the time to train your new hire without needing him to hit the ground running. You must also have the budget to train him and a way to do this, whether it is on-the-job training, informal mentoring, college classes, or some structured training program already in place. If you don't already have this option available, perhaps it is time to consider putting something together for the future.

PREDICTING PERFORMANCE POTENTIAL

Now, with skills sitting on the sideline as a variable that will be decided upon on a job-by-job or company-by-company basis, depending on your individual situation, let's focus on the remaining components of a high performer. What we must address is what to do with the new information we have obtained from a more effective interview: the applicant's locus of control and interest level.

Each of these two components comes with two possible outcomes. For locus of control, the choices are internal and external motivation. For interest level, the choices are passion or the lack of passion for the specific job. Now this combination of choices gives us four possible scenarios. We can have internally or externally motivated applicants whose interests either do or do not mesh with the duties of the job. We can show all four possible combinations on the chart on page 148. Take a look.

Let's expand upon our four possible combinations. Each of the two scales has a midpoint. *All our assessment needs to do is determine on which side of the midpoint an applicant falls for each of the two scales.* The goal of this book is to teach you how to improve your employee selection, not to make it impossible to hire. If you were to look for only a 10 on the locus of control scale and a 100-percent job match on the interest-level scale, you would probably never hire anyone. Because we know that just about everyone falls somewhere in between zero and 10 on each scale, we cannot hold out to hire only applicants who top the scales. This book would not actually improve hiring if it set those expectations. It would instead frustrate a lot of

Motivation-Performance Chart

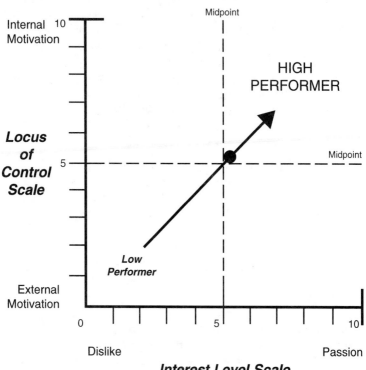

Interest Level Scale

interviewers and make more of a mess out of hiring. And that's certainly not what we need.

So-Called Perfection

We know we have not mastered hiring when we look at some of the employees we have hired who don't even come close to being high performers. Bad hires usually involved incorrect assessment of an applicant's performance potential. Therefore, we can deduce that we are at times also incorrectly assessing the performance potential of the applicants we are not hiring, the ones we turn down. Some of them are quite likely to actually have been good hires. Hiring better does not mean that it has to be more difficult to fill your job openings. Don't envision that your positions will remain unfilled while you keep interviewing, interviewing, and interviewing some more. This is not what it's all about. Sometimes we have the tendency to think the problem with hiring is that we just haven't found the "perfect" employee yet and we must keep looking. The problem also includes the fact that we are incorrectly assessing the performance potential of the applicants we interview.

Improving upon hiring does not mean holding out for so-called perfection or finding a needle in a haystack. Predicting future job performance correctly during the interview process in itself improves hiring. It's about interviewing the applicants better. The result will automatically be selection of better employees, meaning you will be hiring those who will do the best job and not hiring those who won't.

Indeed it would be great to hire that "perfect" employee. But remember: "Perfect" is relative and is contingent upon the job match with an applicant. Ideally we want to hire someone who is predominantly internally motivated and who has a passion for doing that particular job. And if that person has the right skills for the job, what a great combination this is. It's the best, in fact.

EMPLOYING A POWERFUL ATTITUDE

We know that it's a high interest level that motivates a person. When the job duties match with what motivates an applicant, that means he is motivated to do this particular job. Now add to this the "I can" attitude, which believes that a solution can be found and that effort has a direct impact on results, and voila! "I'm interested, I really want to do the job, and I strongly believe that I can accomplish results despite the obstacles that I may be up against," the applicant says. It is a powerful attitude to employ. It's that of a high performer, and the bottom line is that this person will produce more results.

In every workshop, here is when I get a "yeah-but" question. The question is, "What about the working environment. What if it's not conducive for someone to achieve maximum performance?" It truly is a good question, but understand a couple of things here. First of all, there is no perfect work environment. Every job in every company has its share of problems, imperfections, obstacles, and adversities. What you must also realize is that high performers are working in these environments, too, alongside the average and below-average performers. In these imperfect environments, you still have people who produce more results and those who produce less. The high performers are achieving more results in spite of their environment.

It is the externally motivated employee who makes obstacles his excuse for being unable to achieve results. Here again, I'm not saying that these adversities aren't real barriers and that they don't pose a dilemma or need resolving. I fully realize that some work environments stifle productivity and others encourage or enhance job performance. But you need to switch sides here and use this information rather than empathize with the applicant. Use this as an opportunity to determine at what point the applicant stopped trying or whether he even tried at all. Look at how much effort he has put or is currently putting in or how readily he offers up her environment as the excuse for his lack of achievement. It's not the obstacle that stops a person; it's the person's thinking regarding the obstacle that stops him. The obstacle itself has no power, authority, or control over anyone. People give obstacles power when they mentally relinquish their control over them.

I know this may not be the most popular thing to say to everyone, but it is good information and it is true. It may help to remind you here that when you are assessing locus of control, one example or situation is not a pattern and should not lead to a conclusion. It's only when we see a pattern of this behavior that we should become concerned about it. One bad situation or one bad environment won't throw off this assessment. The caution should occur when there is a predominant pattern noticed, one that regularly blames the lack of results on something external or beyond control over and over again. It's not the opportunity that makes a person. Rather, it's what a person does with it. You can give anyone lots of opportunity, but if he does nothing with it, it won't make much of a difference. There have been many disadvantaged people who have succeeded despite the lack of opportunity, just as there are those who have squandered opportunities handed to them on a silver platter. People often want to think it is the lack of opportunity that has caused them to fail, but that's really not so at all.

Hopefully you realize by now that of the four possible combinations, only one involves both components above the midpoint:

the high performer. The three remaining combinations create performance levels less than that of a high performer. They all involve the area below the midpoint on at least one if not both of the scales. Each time you lessen the quantity of any individual part of the components of motivation, you lessen the total output. Mathematically you cannot subtract without affecting the total. Once you reduce one of the components, you cannot have the same level of performance you had when both of these powerful performance influences were higher.

Each of the two parts that make up self-motivation has its own role. When the two are added together you have more, and when some is taken away you have less. You cannot take out or reduce one of these pieces and still have the same level of performance. It doesn't matter which one you reduce. Even though they each have a different impact, you still end up with less in motivation, performance, and results—and not a high performer.

Go for the high performer! It really is the only way to build the best team, the best department, and the best company. Don't settle for less unless you absolutely have to.

WHEN TO COMPROMISE AND HIRE THE NEXT-BEST

When it comes to hiring, I know what you are up against in the real world. I know that you don't want to settle for less and that you want to hire a high performer every time. But realistically, you're not always going to find the highest performers in every pool of applicants. Sometimes your best decision is going to be to compromise. When that happens, you need to do so on your own terms. You need to hire the best possible option for your needs. How do you know when to do that and how to do it effectively?

To make a good decision involving compromise, it is an absolute must that all of the applicants interviewed for the job were accurately assessed first. Many interviewers incorrectly think that they are hiring a high performer and don't find out the real truth until after their new employee is on board. Evaluating the need to compromise was skipped or missed because the applicant wasn't assessed correctly in the first place.

Let's talk about your different hiring options that involve compromising and hiring people who are not high performers. The applicants in these options fall into three categories:

- Internal motivation without passion for the job.
- External motivation with passion for the job.
- External motivation without passion for the job.

Let's discuss each compromise option individually and I'll explain the pros and cons. You may be surprised to find out that there is not one option or compromise that will be the right decision every time or for every job.

OPTION 1:

INTERNAL MOTIVATION WITHOUT PASSION

Just because this option is mentioned first, please do not think that it is a better choice than any of the other compromise options. It very well could be or it may not be. It will depend on what is most important for your hiring needs.

Now, I want you to take a moment and think about an applicant who is internally motivated but lacks passion for his work. What type of locus of control responses will he provide most during your interview? I bet you like the responses that you hear. And what about when you survey his interests? If you do this right and don't provide too much up-front information and don't lead the applicant to the answers you want to hear, how closely do you think the applicant's interests will resemble the duties and responsibilities of your job opening? Here, performance clues are awaiting you.

We have an applicant who has the right attitude to achieve, but the problem is that his interests do not correspond very much with the responsibilities of the job. The "I want to" part of his motivation is undersupplied. This applicant is internally motivated, so he is already equipped with the "find a way" attitude, however, *only* when a person *wants* to find a way will he find one. This applicant's "want to" is low compared with that of an internally motivated person who is passionate about this same job. Will this lesser interest have an effect on motivation or job performance? Absolutely, and you know this now!

This applicant often looks like a great hire because his "I can" attitude has a nice ring, especially if he possesses the right job skills. You just finished interviewing him and you are thinking, *What could be more perfect? There is something I really like about his attitude, it's great, and he has the perfect skills, too.* So you hire him.

You're thinking that there is no better hire, but what you may not realize is that there actually is. This better hire may not exist within your current pool of applicants, but she does exist. Let's look more closely. What exactly does this employee look like performance-wise? If she has the necessary skills, technically she'll be able to do the job. The right attitude is in place so she knows how to overcome obstacles and adversity. She thinks in terms of "possibility." But *what* motivates her is something other than what is involved in this job. What kicks her motivation into high gear is different—or, more specifically, absent—in this job. She may be an average performer, but she is not a high performer. Remember: We cannot subtract from the components that make up motivation and still expect to have the same high level of motivation that is present in a high performer.

If the job consists mainly of this employee's dislikes, this will more than likely de-energize him and procrastination will be a common side effect. Like it or not, accept it or not, I'm just telling you how motivation works. In our workshop, attendees often speak up and give examples of coworkers who fit each of the scenarios. I'm sure you can do the same if you think about people you have worked with or supervised. It can be very frustrating because we know these people have the potential and the ability to do a great job, but we can see that something is holding them back. In this case, it's personal interest or passion, or basically the desire to do the specific job.

Now, when an applicant happens to lack the necessary skills to do the job, this changes things. Let me caution you here regarding this hiring—warning. Think about this for a moment. Imagine having to teach a new employee a job task or skill that he has very little interest of his own to learn. If you have been in management for even a short period of time, this vision already flirts with frustration. Mentally compare the lack of interest and attention of this person with someone who is enthralled with what he has the opportunity to learn. It's a

night-and-day difference in the effect it has on a person's level of motivation to learn. Even a great trainer cannot train a bad hire into being a
great hire.

Guess what? We haven't even discussed the biggest problem that
comes with this scenario or combination yet. What do you think you
get when you combine the ability to put oneself into motion along
with being in a mismatched, unfulfilling, unsatisfying job? The answer
is you have someone who will eventually put himself right into motion, because he is internally motivated, to leave this mismatched job
to find one that's better for him. His next job will be more enjoyable,
more fulfilling, more rewarding, more likeable, more something, or
more of all of these. This is your classic career-changer and often one
of your shorter-term employees. People like him leave jobs sooner
than those people who love what they do because they have no connection to the job; it's absent. When the going gets tough, they often
get going—right out the door. They move on because they have little
reason to stay. They have no love for doing the job. What bond do
they have to keep them there—collecting a paycheck? Yeah, that's a
vision of a high performer. You realize that was only a joke, right?

There is a very strong chance, especially in an industry or profession where there are more job openings than there are people to fill
them, that unhappy employees are just turnover statistics waiting to
happen. It doesn't matter how recently or how long ago they were
hired. People do move on from jobs that they are unhappy with. And
the truth is they also have been known to take jobs that pay less money
but fulfill their passion. Passion is powerful!

Here is where the degree or numbers on both of the scales may
come in handy. Whether the applicant has the skills to do the job or not,
the more he dislikes doing the job or the more it doesn't satisfy him *and*
the more internally motivated he is, then the shorter the duration he's
likely to stay. Also, the greater he dislikes the job, the greater it will affect
job performance.

This is probably a good time to remind you that skills are not
personal motivators; they are merely enablers. So therefore the presence of skills doesn't indicate job interests or job satisfaction. Skills
don't necessarily parallel with an applicant's personal interests or goals.
Don't make the mistake of assuming that just because an applicant
applies for the job he is passionate about or even likes doing that type

of work. You must accurately uncover the applicant's authentic interests. You could end up hiring an applicant who has sufficient skills to do the job but insufficient interest to be fully motivated to do it well.

Even though we may not classify this person as a high performer, I don't want to say that this applicant is always a bad hire, because he is not. There are several variables you should look at first before you come to this conclusion. Ask yourself the following questions:

- During the interview, did the applicant mention one time or did it come out several times how much he dislikes certain tasks?
- How severe is the mismatch between the job and the applicant's interests?
- Are those tasks critical to this job? Or is it maybe only a slight mismatch where it's almost a 50-50 toss-up with some of both the applicant's likes and dislikes involved in the job?

What we want to ascertain here before you do consider moving ahead with this compromise is how severe is the mismatch? Now that you know the impact a job mismatch has on job performance, the question should be why would you want to hire an applicant who has already directly or indirectly admitted to not enjoying what this job involves? There have to be other good reasons to hire.

Even though there definitely is an area for concern here, this might still be a satisfactory hiring choice. If internal motivation is predominant and the mismatch isn't too drastic, it could be okay. If the needed skills are present so that training is not required, and if filling the job right away is critical, and if there are no signs of an impending career change, you may easily have an average job performer. In many cases and in many very tight labor markets, having the job filled with an average job performer is much better than keeping the job open.

This scenario usually isn't the one that involves bottomed-out poor performance, because this combination still has some good things going for it. When you see a predominant mode of operation that encourages achievement, the job mismatch is only slight, and skills are present, you definitely could do worse—and you probably have.

Because we have defined a high performer as someone who achieves more results, every compromise choice will involve job performance that is ranked below that of a high performer. Because the goal of this book is to teach you how to better identify high performers, once you realize that none of your applicants is likely to be a top performers, then you must decide whether this one is a good compromise choice for your hiring situation.

OPTION 2:
EXTERNAL MOTIVATION WITH CAREER FIT

Okay, the rules just changed here with this one. We just swapped everything and have made it the complete opposite applicant. Instead of internal motivation, we have an externally motivated applicant. And instead of missing the passion, we've got it now in this applicant. Stop for a moment and think about this combination. I'll bet if you try doing this before reading on, you can figure out what the issues will be with this one.

Well, to start with, having the passion piece is wonderful. With it comes the energy to conquer the world. It has been said that nothing big has ever been accomplished without passion. People make things happen because they have passion. With or without skills, this person can be a great protégé who is willing to learn more about something that already interests him.

Still, with all the power of passion, where we run into trouble with this combination is that the person comes with a fully formed, fully established way of thinking that is not conducive to finding solutions and conquering obstacles effectively. Here, the attitude conducive for achievement is in short supply. It's not predominant.

This applicant's thinking more often comes to the conclusion that many obstacles are simply insurmountable. Sometimes he is absolutely convinced of this and there is no telling him otherwise. These are the "it's someone else's fault, not mine" or the "why bother to try because it will never work?" people.

How does this play out on the job? Let's stop here for a minute so I can point out that for this to play out on the job at all, this person had to have been hired first. In the past, this assessment has been excluded from the hiring decision. It's almost amazing to think about how much we have been missing when it comes to making good decisions simply because as interviewers we didn't know what to seek. We can't say that anymore.

Because of his predominant "I can't" attitude, this employee does not always put himself into motion when and where he could. This is how he differs from a high performer. When he disconnects himself from outcomes, he is relinquishing his own power and giving it to the external world. He also automatically relinquishes his attitude and belief in his own potential and ability. Absent of the perception of control, this person doesn't fully realize or actualize his own potential. He doesn't always *go for it* and he doesn't always *give it his all*. His "I can't" thinking stops him before he ever gets started or very shortly after. Because it is thought that governs action, if the thought doesn't believe that personal action will have any impact on results, then it deduces that there is no rational reason to expend the effort.

When it comes to hiring, you might be surprised that there is both good news and bad news with this combination. The good news is that when internal motivation is lacking, there is a substitute. Instead of "self," motivation can be induced by something external of self such as a supervisor. Essentially, you light a fire under him, whether through discipline, threat of job loss, or something more on a positive note such as incentives, rewards, or just plain verbal inspiration. The downside to having to motivate employees is that it has limitations. It lasts only as long as the external motivator is hot. Hiring externally motivated employees requires much more time and energy after the hire. The time spent managing and motivating them could be better spent on other management tasks. You also must realize that you probably are not going to change these employees. What you hire is what you get. Mentoring and offering a positive influence are good, but permanent change is strictly up to them and usually much easier said than done. When your influence wears off, it will need to be reapplied and nothing actually will have changed. Looking at the bright side here, at least there is a substitute—unlike passion, which has none.

Let's think about the job for a moment. Not every job may require a high level of internal motivation. And not all jobs require a lot of obstacle conquering. Be careful, however, of what you think of as an obstacle. It could be something as simple as dealing with a difficult coworker and not just a Mount Everest–sized problem.

Also realize that external motivation is not an assessment or a label about someone's character. These people are just as smart, honest, nice, and dependable as everyone else is or isn't. This is merely a very narrowly focused assessment involving perception of personal control. The truth is you already have many externals in productive jobs right now. They are not unemployable; they are just not the highest performers. I am not saying not to ever hire them; I am saying you should know what performance level you are dealing with as you make the choice to hire or not to hire. Accurately assess your applicants and don't get surprised.

Probably the most common side effect plaguing the externally motivated person is constricted thinking. This thinking limits solutions, is problem-focused, involves excessive blaming or excuse-making, and includes a victim or entitlement mentality, all because of a lack of perceived control. It might sound pretty terrible when you put it like that, and you're thinking, *Why would I want to hire this type of person?* These side effects have to do with conquering and moving beyond the obstacles that are in the way, and this type of thinking does affect job results. Performance will not be zero, but it will be less than that of high performer when you compare the two. You must be able to see this difference ahead of time, before you make your decision to hire.

Many jobs do not require employees to go out and slay dragons. An example would be any job that had a lot of structure in place. It has specific procedures spelled out that dictate how to handle most every situation encountered. And if a situation should occur outside of the spelled-out guidelines, then someone else with higher authority would be available to handle it. An example of this may be a cashier job in a department store that deals with merchandise returns. If the return-policy procedures are clearly defined, creative problem-solving may not be a necessity for this job to be done well. It would still be ideal to hire a high performer for this job, but it would not be the end of the world to compromise and hire someone whose passion fit the job and who only needed perhaps a little bit of external motivation.

Someone once told me that the main difference between an internal and an external computer programmer was that when an external found a problem he would take it to his boss to solve. He would drop the problem in the boss's lap without thinking through how it could be solved. The internal, on the other hand, perceiving less limitation and being more open to solutions, would expand his thinking until he came up with the best answer. Then, if need be, he would take the solution to his boss for approval. It's similar to the difference between being reactive and proactive: The latter one finds a solution.

External motivation comes in degrees, and so does internal motivation. As you start to incorporate the gathering of this information into your interview process, you will begin to see the differences between applicants. Right at this moment, without having put this information or these interviewing techniques to work, you cannot know for sure what I am talking about. But you will. And as you do, you will notice that some applicants provide many more excuses than others do and these applicants will no longer be able to conceal their lack of effort to achieve what they say they want to achieve. Whether you hear a lot of excuses, some excuses, or only one or two, you will soon be able to use this to compare applicants to each other and estimate just how internally or externally motivated they are. It is simply more information that gives you the opportunity to make better hiring decisions.

If you hire someone who is externally motivated, that does not mean you will have a problem employee. We are only talking about perceived control. Passion has a magical way of motivating even those who were previously unmotivated in jobs that didn't interest them. Employees can be mediocre just because they lack interest in what they are doing. Switch them to an area that sparks their attention and watch the upswing in motivation.

Here are a few questions you'll need to answer before you can decide whether this is a good compromise:

- Does the job require much creative problem-solving and obstacle-hurdling in order for the employee to be successful?
- Does the job already have good structure or procedures in place or a good support system that can offer guidance and solutions?
- How externally motivated is the applicant?
- As a supervisor, do you have the time to light a fire and keep it burning under this employee—in other words, to be his external motivator?

Often I refer to this applicant as the "High Performance Imposter" because if he has the needed skills and can talk the lingo, he can often fool interviewers into thinking he is a better job performer than he actually is. As an interviewer, you focus on his enthusiasm and his passion, missing the fact that his attitude toward achievement is lacking. You don't hear those excuses for what they really are, and you make the judgment call that they are legitimate. If the applicant is interview-savvy, he knows he needs to pick out as many of his past success stories as possible and talk them up to you. Now that you know about Motivation-Based Interviewing, however, you are better equipped. You can ask more effective interview questions utilizing the O-SAE Method and can see through isolated or occasional examples to determine the more consistent behavior that lies just underneath this façade. Trust me: If it exists, it's there. If you don't see it, it's because you missed it, not because it wasn't present.

Whatever decision you make here, you need to base it on sound applicant information. And if you do this well, the performance level you think you are hiring and what you actually get will be one and the same. Again, every compromise depends on each job, and there is no one right or wrong one, just a best one for your particular job opening at that time. Hiring someone who is externally motivated but very interested in the work won't fill your job opening with a high performer, but it may perhaps be a very good compromise under the right conditions.

Option 3:
External Motivation Without Career Fit

I'll go ahead and tell you that this is the only person I will recommend that you never hire. The whole reason this scenario even exists at some workplaces is because interviewers select the wrong people to do a job. In fact, they select an applicant with low self-motivation to do a job that doesn't bolster his motivation level, which diminishes it more. Then to aggravate the situation, managers try to correct bad hiring by trying to change the employee and make him into something that he is not, something the managers should have hired in the first place. This combination would be nonexistent if employers put externally motivated people only into jobs that matched their interests.

Even though this combination doesn't have to exist, it does. I would love to pretend that it didn't, but we need to go ahead and address it. It will benefit you to know the information about this combination. When you combine an externally motivated applicant with a poorly matched job, you get a double negative. This double negative really zaps motivation and shears job performance. In fact, this combination results in the lowest performance level.

In a tight labor market, everyone who wants to be employed is working. As obvious as that may seem, what you may not realize is that low job performers are being hired all the time, but usually not on purpose. Many of them can interview well. They easily slip in by fooling untrained interviewers or interviewers who are not paying close enough attention.

What we have here, just as with the previous scenario, is an externally motivated applicant. But this time the passion for the job is lacking. As with the High Performance Imposter, this applicant can tell you about a time or two when he finished a tough project, showed initiative, and had success. These examples, however, will be limited in number. Using Motivation-Based Interviewing and determining predominant responses instead of using only individual answers to determine a conclusion will help you to see this better than you have in the past. If you continually ask obstacle-related questions to an externally motivated person, it won't be long before he will be forced to make excuses and blame others for various situations. His success stories will only go so far, and you're going to go beyond that place to assess his overall predominant attitude. Just keep asking questions that involve adversity. Trust me: Most of the time you will clearly be able to see the difference between the attitudes of internally and externally motivated applicants.

In this last scenario now, you have an applicant who is predominantly an excuse-maker who feels he has little control to affect outcomes. To compound matters, he lacks interest in what he is doing. He may even be blaming his boss or his company for this whole situation. I know you've seen or heard these employees. This is the customer-service rep who avoids dealing with customers as much as he can get away with and then makes excuses for this behavior if confronted. This is the accounts-receivable clerk who never takes the initiative to look up posting codes in a reference book given to her and instead constantly interrupts her boss to ask for this information. She never takes responsibility for learning but is quick to blame others when confronted, saying she wasn't trained properly. This is the call-center manager who would rather fight with a customer and say there is nothing that can be done, that it's out of his control, than find a solution that would be a win-win and would retain the customer. Shall I go on? And don't forget that all these people had to go through a job interview before being hired.

And one more thing: This is the one employee you wish would just quit and move on, but he is not even motivated to do this until he gets an external push to put him into motion or until leaving becomes the path of least resistance. Only when it becomes easier to leave than it is to stay will this person take the initiative to find another job.

Sometimes interviewers get so stuck on hiring skills they miss all the other great information available. In their defense, perhaps the company is not set up to train new employees who lack skills but who otherwise are highly motivated. Skills become a blinding factor. Working for other companies myself, I have had to unnecessarily settle for less than a high performer because of this stigma behind skills. They are often thought of as the be-all and end-all when it comes to superior job performance. But they are not. As I have said throughout this book, there is more to selecting a high performer than hiring only those applicants who happen to have the perfect skill set, at exactly the perfect time of your job opening.

In this third scenario, even if you provide the external push needed to motivate the employee, realize that you are trying to put him into motion to do something he dislikes doing. There will be resistance to motion here because of his lack of interest. If you've ever heard of "shadow hiring" or "the warm body syndrome," this is it. You put an applicant under a bright light and if he casts a shadow, you hire him. Or if he can fog a mirror with his breathing, you hire him. In other words, being alive makes him qualified. He just fills an opening—no more than that. I may make a joke about it, but this situation is a lose-lose for everyone involved, and that's not funny.

Because motivation will be at its lowest point with this applicant, it really doesn't matter that much whether this person possesses the right skills. I cannot recommend this scenario primarily because this book is about hiring high performers, but also because you can do a lot better.

No Compromise

Let's talk about one more option available to you other than what we have discussed: choosing not to compromise. You have the option to keep your job opening unfilled while you continue the search. If you didn't have a high performer within your first group of applicants, keep interviewing. As long as you have the time, budget, and resources to do this, why settle?

Hiring well requires that you put the work in on the front end in order to have the highest payoff on the back end. You may get lucky once in a while and hire a high performer without putting in this effort, but in the long run this won't pay off for you. If you don't do everything you need to do to hire great employees, if you shortchange the process, you will end up shortchanging yourself. The trade-off is having to motivate the unmotivated—yes, the ones that you hired.

Every job opening is an opportunity to build the best team. If you have the "hurry up and hire so I can get back to my own work" attitude, there's a strong chance you'll actually make more work for yourself, not less. You thought you were saving time or didn't have the time, but guess what? You're not. You must put the work and attention into the front end of the hiring process. You must learn as much as you can about how to master the interview process. That is when you will be able to hire the best. It should be starting to make sense about now and explain the reason for those great and not-so-great hires in your past.

CHAPTER 12

TAKING HIRING
TO THE NEXT LEVEL

The number-one reason for reading this book is to improve hiring. Hiring an employee is akin to entering into a marriage. It is a relationship between employee and employer that you want to turn out happily-ever-after. But how can it if we start this union by selecting a work partner who is not a good match? From there we wonder what went wrong as if it is some big mystery that will never be solved. Get real! We got the exact hiring outcome that we did because of the applicant *we* selected to be our employee.

During an interview, believing an applicant would do a great job and would be a great hire doesn't make it so. And when we select someone who turns out to be not so great, we have the tendency to say our selection process is fine and the employee was the problem. Let's take another look.

The problem here often isn't what we think it is, meaning solely the employee's performance. Aren't you leaving out the selection process that allowed a poor performer to be hired in the first place? If you could hire anyone without absolutely any worry, there would be no issue with how well the selection process worked or not. But that's not the case.

It is time for us to stop ignoring this area. Every company should be great at selecting its human capital. Employers should do this better than they do almost anything else. Hiring can be greatly improved with just a little work, and you can begin seeing results right away. The investment has such a tremendous impact on the company's bottom line. Wait no longer.

Ask yourself this: If you would have known in advance of hiring a poor performer, "in advance" meaning that you determined this during the interview, would you still have hired that person? The employee cannot take sole responsibility here. You own the responsibility of extending a job offer to those who turn out to be poor performers. It is the same as taking credit for a great hire. You must take responsibility for all of your hires, good and bad. Shedding the responsibility that is yours here automatically blocks the learning that needs to take place in order for you to take hiring to the next level. If there is nothing you believe you did to make a bad hire, then there is nothing for you to change or improve upon. If something outside of you, or something outside the control you believe you have, caused this situation, then only that which you believe has the control can cause change. This leaves you off the hook—or so you think. And with that thinking, the cycle repeats and hiring never improves.

BAD HIRES

As an interviewer, you should realize that hiring well is not just about reading this book and jumping into your next interview with expectations of great hiring absent of any hiring mistakes. Your expectations should be realistic. I've seen it countless times. Interviewers brag about their hiring success stories, completely excluding those hires that failed. Trust me: I know we all have those people we wish we hadn't hired. You cannot include only good hires when evaluating your own personal interviewing skill and ability. Then you would feel you have already mastered this process and that you had no need or room to improve. And along with that type of thinking, no improvement will occur. Did I mention yet in this book that attitude is just about everything? That includes yours.

Bad hires cannot be attributed to things out of one's control or blamed on others involved in the selection process. For interviewers to truly learn to interview better and ultimately how to hire better employees, they must perceive having control over the outcome of the hiring process. As much as we talk about this, here we are still talking about predicting the future performance of people we barely know in most cases. It can feel as if we have little control as interviewers. Here is where you must really begin. You must change *your* thinking.

Substandard interviewing produces substandard hiring. For those hires that we have done well, we truly did predict good performance in advance. But we must become more consistent with this end result and reduce the number of hires that miss the target. This is possible. There absolutely are those people who are better at hiring and those who are not. It is not this great mystery or psychology art form that can be mastered by only a select few. You, too, can hire high performers.

NO SURPRISES!

Here's how it works. This is how you know when you are really getting good at hiring. I call it the *Two Minutes in Two Months Checkup*. It is a recap or a mental review of your interviewing results or determination. It is a comparison between the pre-hire performance prediction and the post-hire performance results. You are comparing the performance level that you thought you were going to get with the performance level that you actually got—predicted outcome versus actual outcome.

You see, after what you read about compromising in the previous chapter, you should realize that making a good hiring decision might involve knowingly hiring someone who is not a high performer but is still your best applicant. A better definition of a good hire is really when there is no surprise between who you think you are hiring and who you actually do hire, job performance–wise. Improving hiring involves correctly assessing future job performance.

For several different reasons, we have a tendency to more often overrate applicants than to underrate them. If their performance turns out to be different than what we predicted, oftentimes it turns out to be not as good as we thought and rarely does it turn out to be much better than we were expecting. Hence, we overrated them. When this variance occurs, it is not in our favor.

As long as there is a variance between our interview determination about future performance and the actual future performance, our interview is flawed and has room for improvement. Here is my challenge to you: After you have hired someone and that person has been on the job about two months, do a quick mental assessment about her overall job performance. Is she doing better than expected, as expected, or less than expected? Now, think back to your interview with this person. Two months is not too long to remember some details. Did you peg this person exactly? If yes, how did you do this? What was it that you picked up on? If you were somewhere between pretty close and exactly on target regarding future job performance, pat yourself on the back. You did a great job! Reinforce what you picked up on so you can repeat this success. Etch it into your mind. Whatever you did, turn it into a habit if it isn't already.

If you missed the mark in either direction—if the applicant turned out to be better than or not as good as you expected—challenge yourself to think back and uncover what you may have missed. The goal is to gather relevant applicant information that accurately predicts how that applicant will perform in the future. With that information, you decide whether to hire and, in many cases, whether to compromise. If your information is useless for predicting future performance, then you will be basing your decision on irrelevant information.

Even if you accidentally ended up with a great hire, this doesn't take you off the hook. The goal is to conduct an interview and gather the information that consistently represents future performance, not to rely on luck. Unfortunately, luck comes in two packages, not just one. Where there is good luck, there can also be bad luck, and that's not good enough when it comes to hiring.

GREAT INTERVIEWERS

To become great at hiring, you must challenge yourself. When you hire well, congratulate yourself and reinforce what you did right. And then keep doing that. When you don't hire so well, use the experience as a learning opportunity. Try to figure out what you missed. What did you perhaps pick up on but then discount because you didn't think it was important? Hindsight can often be the greatest teacher. With the employee's current performance in mind, ask yourself where you would have been able to pick this up or where clues would have been visible. Would it have been during skills, locus of control, or interest level assessment? This mental conversation *must* take place; otherwise, your skill level as an interviewer will remain the same—and worse, your hiring mistakes will continue to occur. The trick to knowing when you are getting really good at interviewing and hiring is not when you are hiring only high performers. Instead it's when you accurately and consistently predict the performance of each applicant you hire.

Let me give you an example of what I mean here. Many years ago, I was asked to help out in a crisis-hiring situation by a company that was a seasonal business and did about 80 percent of its entire year's sales between October and December. It was mid-October, and the company suddenly was without a manager in a store in Salt Lake City.

I did not have the time to actually go out there to help. I told the company to call an employment agency to find applicants quickly, narrow down the field, and then I would conduct a full-length interview via phone from Atlanta. Then the company could have someone out there conduct an in-person interview—which I always recommend.

During my interview with the candidate, it was determined that this person—the only one found on short notice—could do the job and had prior skills and experience but wasn't highly motivated. When the applicant and I talked about his skills and about his day-to-day job responsibilities, it came out that he was more externally motivated than internally motivated. While assessing his interest level, I discovered he was taking night classes in a completely different career field and would be finishing up in just a few months. The applicant said he really liked the idea that this job would not interfere with his classes, and therefore he was very interested in the job.

When I spoke with the company, this is what I relayed to the hiring officials: I believe the applicant has the necessary skills and would be able to perform the job. However, he is externally motivated. If hired, he would need to be motivated by someone or something other than himself—in other words, he'd have to have a fire lit under him. In this job, do not expect him to dazzle you with stellar performance. Oh, and one more thing: I expect that he would not stay more than six months before making a career change.

Remember that the company was in a crisis-hiring situation and had no other viable applicants. Basically the company was out of time. What we had here was probably an average-performing skilled employee at best who most likely wouldn't stay very long. Even though the company's options were not looking too good, it wasn't the end of the world. One thing in its favor in this situation was that this applicant did have the necessary skills to do the job. That was important here because there was no time to train anyone for this position. In somewhat of a quandary, the company wasn't sure what to do. I asked, "If this applicant could get you through the busy season and performed only average or perhaps slightly below and then he quit, would that be okay?" The answer to that was yes.

This applicant was hired. He stayed five months and did move on to another career field, the one that matched the college classes he was taking. The company got through its busy season without any major problems in that store. Was this, in fact, a bad hire because the applicant wasn't a high performer? Absolutely not! It was a good hiring decision under the circumstances. What is key here is that what the company thought it was going to get is the same as what it did get. A hiring decision was based on information that accurately predicted future performance. There was no surprise about performance or tenure in this case; therefore, a good decision was made. In order to make a good decision on compromising when it comes to hiring, you must know what the compromise involves.

SELLING THE APPLICANT

Let's take some time to talk about the other side of the coin. It is a very important topic, because you cannot successfully hire high performers without knowing this next piece. Being able to accurately distinguish a high performer from one pretending to be during the interview is not all there is to hiring the best. Spotting them does not guarantee hiring them. Hiring involves both extending a job offer and an "yes, I'll take it" response from the applicant.

You can want the applicant, but the applicant also needs to want you, or else the deal will not work out. There is a good chance your applicant, the one you want to hire, is interviewing with more companies than just yours. He could even be interviewing with your competitors. And just to let you know, if your competitors have trained interviewers, then they, too, know this applicant is a good one to hire. You had better cross your fingers and hope your applicant likes your job or your company a little more than he likes the others.

But, in truth, you don't have to leave this to hope, luck, or chance—something external. There is an influential power you have, and you probably are unaware of it. I'm talking about selling the applicant on the job, but I am not talking about doing this via traditional means. Most interviewers make two very big mistakes with this part of the process. First, they wait until the end of the round of interviews until they have decided which applicant they want to hire and then they begin selling the job to just that one applicant. Secondly, they use the same canned sales presentation every time on all applicants. For example:

> *"We are a 40-year-old, stable Fortune 500 company. We are growing at almost 10 percent annually. We offer competitive compensation and have a great benefits package. Our benefits include medical and dental insurance, a 401(k), educational reimbursement, a liberal vacation policy, sick leave, and paid time off."*

If you yourself as an applicant heard the preceding information, how enticed would you now be to accept the job with that company? The answer isn't necessarily "I'm not interested," but it also isn't necessarily an excited "yes!" The only way this pitch will sell an applicant on a job or on a company is if it contains information that is important to that particular applicant. Think about it: If education reimbursement is not important to you because you are finished with school, then that is not a selling point to you. On the other hand, if you are trying to finish your master's degree and have been wondering how to pull this off financially, all of a sudden this is a *big* plus to you.

HOT BUTTONS

To find the selling points for an applicant, you must discover his "hot buttons," or pieces of information that will have impact on his decision. These hot buttons are personal and have meaning to only that one particular applicant. You can tell all applicants about the wonderful things about a job or a company, but if those things have no meaning or are unimportant to them, you are no further ahead than if you had said nothing.

Middle management across Corporate America seems to think there is only one hot button and that it's money—the paycheck or salary offer. Not so at all! The reason for this belief is that when employees leave a job and move on to another one, they often state their reason for leaving is for more money. Realize that this is a standard courtesy answer, one that is generic, is perfectly acceptable, and doesn't burn any bridges—but it is also not the whole story.

I know you don't want to instantly believe what I'm telling you, but think about it. If the employee was making the same pay since his last performance evaluation, which was, let's say, six months ago, and he started job hunting one month ago, something else initiated that action. If pay were the real issue, why was this person not job hunting two or three months or really five months ago? Something else triggered him to start job hunting at this particular time and you should probe further to get more details. He may be seeking more money where he is going, but it's standard practice to offer more money to a new hire than he was making at his prior job.

By using the selling techniques I'm about to show you, I have personally extended many job offers for less money than applicants were making in their prior jobs. I wasn't low-balling the applicants. In each case, I would have loved to pay them more, but it just wasn't in the budget. However, I didn't want that to stop me from hiring the best. I still wanted them to say yes! Trust me: There are many more reasons than pay for why people leave old jobs and accept new ones. You have to learn what those reasons are for each applicant and sell back to those points.

There is really good news here. Without even realizing it, by using Motivation-Based Interviewing, you have learned what the applicant's hot buttons are or, more specifically, an effective way to sell the applicant on your job. You picked up that information about the applicant while assessing his interests, likes, dislikes, strengths, weaknesses, and goals.

The information plays a dual role. You are already using it to compare the applicant's compatibility with the job and assess his motivation to do it. Now you can provide corresponding job and company information that complements the applicant's likes, strengths, and goals. And you can use the information you picked up about his dislikes and weaknesses to tell him about the limited exposure that the job would involve in those areas. But let me make one point very clear right here: *You must represent the job honestly and accurately.* Doing anything else will have negative ramifications. The bottom line is that the applicant will still quit and/or performance will suffer if he gets into a job he doesn't like. Selling a job through rose-colored glasses doesn't change the individual into liking a job that doesn't fit him. Instead, it makes a bigger mess.

An applicant has to provide some reason for leaving a job. For example, let's say the applicant mentions he left a prior job because he disliked being micromanaged all the time. He likes having some autonomy. And let's say your company's environment would give him some decision-making power. Sell that fact back to him at that moment. Say, "In this environment you will have autonomy. No one will be standing over you questioning your every move...." If the applicant mentions that he likes something in particular from a prior job and that factor exists in your job, mention it to him right when you find this out.

If the applicant has exceptional organization skills as a strength and you know how badly you need that in this job, mention that to him. Tell him how wonderful it would be to have someone who could come in and organize the place. Tell him he would be great. People shine when they can flash their talents and strengths. Imagine this person going home from the interview and telling his spouse, "I know I could do a great job for company XYZ. They could really use someone who has my kind of strengths. I would be really good at that job." He has already started thinking of himself in that role, which might make him a little more likely to accept your job offer later instead of someone else's. It's that simple.

TIMING IS EVERYTHING!

This now brings me back to the first mistake I mentioned that interviewers commonly make: Waiting too long to start selling applicants on the job. Generally you might be thinking that you don't start selling until you have decided you want to hire a particular applicant. Wrong! That's too late. By the end of your process or by the time you have made up your mind that you want to hire someone, that person may already be leaning in a different direction toward a different company. You have absolutely nothing to lose by selling every applicant early on. The worst that happens is that you have more applicants interested in the job than you have positions to offer. That is much better than having no one interested—especially your top candidate.

It's never too early to start selling an applicant on your job. Ideally, this process will begin way before you even know you want to hire this person. It also means you will sell the job to many applicants you will not end up hiring. Keeping these potential employees interested is a very important step in the selection process.

One word of caution, however: Many interviewers want to tell applicants all about the job, their expectations, what they are looking for, and what they aren't looking for all in the beginning of the interview. They think this gets the interview off to a right start and helps everyone when the applicant knows what information to pull out of his background. No, no, no! Because of *The Interview Relationship*, applicants will take this information and use it to provide "right" answers. Many applicants will customize and even alter their answers to tell you what they think you want to hear, all in an attempt to receive a job offer.

Giving information about the job is great. Knowing when to give it and how to give it is much better. You want to provide as much accurate job information as you can to the applicant, but not in a way that hurts you as the interviewer. You don't want the information you provide to negatively affect your job of information-gathering. Giving up-front information is a win for the applicant and often a lose for the interviewer. Selling to the applicant in a way that gets him excited about the job is a win-win. And the most effective way is not a canned spiel but rather a customized version that fits each applicant. Any other information you want to give should be given at the end of the interview after you are finished gathering information about the applicant.

THE INTERVIEW FORMAT

Let's cover the interview format you are using. In Chapter 7 we talked about getting the applicant to let down his guard by starting with small talk at the beginning of the interview before jumping in. That's just the beginning of the overall interview format you must create for yourself to follow. The purpose here is not necessarily to change your current method. There isn't just one and only one format that is effective. Many different interviewing formats work well. But in case you have never established an interviewing structure you are comfortable with or one you feel works well, now is the time to make changes. If you develop a system for conducting an interview, you will place less focus on what to do or ask next and place more focus on listening to the applicant closely. I know that for some, conducting an interview can be as nerve-racking to the interviewer as it is to some applicants. This will help ease that feeling.

Let me tell you about the system that I use that works very well for me. When the applicant first comes in, I like the receptionist to instruct the applicant to fill out an application completely. I do not accept the words *See Resume* written on the application in the employment history section. There are several reasons for this. You would think that when I see those words I could just jump over to the resume and find the exact same information that is being requested on the application, but that's not the case. For example, it's normal to find an applicant's job title, name of employer, list of duties, responsibilities, and accomplishments on the resume. However, other information such as names of supervisors, address, and phone number for each employer, salary information, and dates of employment including the month (not just the year) are all usually requested on an application and are omitted on most resumes. And sometimes those things are left off for a very good reason. As an interviewer who is trying to make the best hiring decision possible, I have the right to know this information, need to know it, and want to know it. There are even legal benefits to having this information about each applicant. And let me add just one more thing: I feel that writing "See Resume" is lazy. Get my point here?

Next, I have the receptionist notify me when the applicant is finished filling out the application and then I go to the lobby and welcome the applicant. If you don't have this kind of set-up, just make sure you keep an eye on the applicant and don't keep him waiting at all if you can prevent it. His time is as valuable to him as yours is to you, and you need to respect that.

There is a good chance that this applicant is meeting you for the very first time at this point. The first step is to make a warm and friendly first impression—even if you are not a warm and friendly type of person. This initial contact is where the applicant assesses how on-guard he should be. If you as the interviewer come across too stern, rigid, or unfriendly, you'll have to work harder at lowering his guard during the interview. Help yourself out here.

Neutral, non-controversial small talk can take place while you and the applicant are walking back to your office. Good topics are the traffic, the ease or difficulty in finding the office, the weather, and so on. Allow your applicant to get settled before you jump in. Relax him by continuing the light conversation until you see some of the nervousness and stiffness within his body language dissipate. This can take one minute or 10, depending on the applicant. It is well worth the time investment because you may end up shooting yourself in the foot by not doing it. It hurts you when your applicant holds back. In fact, you may actually help him to not say some things he might have if he had been more relaxed and felt more at ease with you.

This is about the time when I explain to the applicant the format of the interview. I'll usually say something such as this:

> *"I just want to give you an overview of the interview today. We are going to start by reviewing your work history. I have a set of questions I'll be asking every applicant interviewing for this job. I want to let you know that I take notes so I don't forget anything and sometimes it takes me a moment to do those. Once I'm finished, you'll have an opportunity to ask any questions you may have about the job and I'll be happy to answer them for you. Sound like a plan?"*

I always get a nod to the rhetorical question at the end as a go-ahead for getting started. From there I just follow the plan. I start with past work history. I use the backside of the application, the work history section, as my working guide. I usually start three jobs back and work to the present or most recent job. Of course, it varies depending on the applicant's work history. Sometimes I start with the current job and work back in time. There is nothing significant about doing one over the other. What is significant, however, is the information I gather here. I walk through each job and job change and seek detailed information:

- Why did you take the job?
- At what pay did you take the job?
- What were your duties and responsibilities?
- Did you get promoted?
- If you got promoted, to what position and pay?
- How did your job responsibilities change?
- What did you like best and least about this job?
- When and why did you decide to leave this job?
- Did you give notice and how long?
- Did you work that time period out?

- Did you have your next job waiting before you gave notice?
- What was it about that new job that made you accept it?

I want to understand the big picture and get some details, too. When it comes time to ask skill-assessment questions, now that I know this work history information about the applicant, I will be able to better relate to the past experience examples he will use to answer the questions. It seems as if I am casually reviewing the work record, but I am also really gathering locus of control and interest-level information. Starting with work history is a good way to ease into the interview process because there doesn't appear to be much judgment going on here.

Next it's on to assessing the applicant's skills. This is where you use interview questions you have previously written based on the O-SAE Method. Remember that to be effective, the questions must be designed in advance and asked of the applicant one by one. Have enough spacing in between the questions on your written copy so you can take notes. Write down the highlights of what the applicant says. Write enough so that you can recall his answers later.

Group similar questions together. What I mean here is that you may choose to ask several sets of questions specific to one skill. Talk that topic out. Don't skip around. Don't leave one skill, discuss a different one, and then go back to the first one. Stay with each skill until it's finished and then move on to the next one. I also don't recommend that you rate each individual answer but instead rate the overall skill. No matter how many questions you end up asking for each skill, only have one rating per skill.

Speaking of rating, I like to use a one-through-five score to rate skills—five being best, three meaning average, and one for the worst. Know in advance your expectation for each rating score. Don't liberally hand out fours and fives. The majority of the applicants will not perform this job at that high level if hired and therefore should not be overrated. When we miss the target while selecting employees, we are more often disappointed instead of pleasantly surprised, which we already discussed. This is consistent with overrating, not underrating. Do you have a habit of overrating applicants? Do you need to adjust how you rate them? Give it some thought and make the necessary adjustments.

As you are asking your prepared interview questions, if you think of any follow-up questions, go ahead and ask them. In fact, because you have your core questions written in advance, you will have more mental freedom to think of the probing questions that will need to be asked to ensure clarity on the topic.

Once I'm satisfied with skill assessment, I flow right into the five interest-level questions. They are simple and take only about five minutes. From there I wrap up by turning over the interview to the applicant. Even if I am not very interested in hiring an applicant at this point, I give the courtesy of answering a few of his questions. After all, he spent his time answering mine. If I'm really interested, however, I let the applicant ask as many questions as time allows. I feel it's important for an applicant to be well informed about the job he is considering.

Many years ago, I used to tell interviewers to note what types of issues the applicant was focusing on in his questions, such as benefits, vacation and time-off policy, future promotional opportunities, and company stability. In the past, this would offer the interviewer clues about the applicant's motives. But not anymore, because most applicants are prepared and more interview-savvy than before. Just go to any job-posting site on the Internet. Most of them offer free advice to job seekers. They even provide a list of generic questions for applicants to ask their interviewers so they give a good impression. This advice is right on target and of great benefit to applicants. Don't worry, however. It is okay that an applicant is prepared and able to interview well. Motivation-Based Interviewing will even the playing field by better equipping you, the interviewer, to see through any false fronts.

THE NUMBER-ONE COMPLAINT

Let me finish talking about the interview format by mentioning *timeliness*. It is the number-one complaint I have come across regarding applicants and the hiring process. Timeliness refers to when you get back to the applicant about whether or not you are extending a job offer. Realize that it's a big step for anyone to change jobs. For most of us, our jobs are a big part of our lives. Waiting for a company to decide whether or not it wants to extend an offer can be stressful and can somewhat put the applicant's life temporarily on hold. Applicants are people just like you and me. They don't want you to exceed expectations by getting back to them sooner than you said you would, even though that would be nice. What they really want is for you to just keep your word and give them an answer on time. Honor your promises. It's very frustrating sitting and waiting, especially when the deadline time discussed for having an answer has come and gone with no word.

When you don't give the applicant a timely answer, it doesn't matter that you had good intentions. It doesn't matter that the reference checks didn't get finished in time, that a really important project suddenly got dropped in your lap, or that maybe you were out sick for a day. All that matters is that the candidate is left with a bad impression of you and your company and that if you do decide to extend an offer, you'll have to work a little bit harder to get him to say yes.

Here's my recommendation. The solution is not to lengthen the amount of time you set for giving the applicant an answer. Instead, go ahead and tell him you are still interviewing applicants and hope to have an answer by such and such date. Tell him to call you if he needs to have an answer before he hears from you. Tell him everyone will be notified one way or the other and that if he hasn't heard from you it's because you don't have a decision yet.

Understand something here. In your mind you want to have this position filled by next Tuesday. That's not a start date but when you will make your decision and extend an offer. So you tell every applicant there will be an answer by Tuesday or the first part of next week. Well, let's say you extend the offer to your first-choice candidate and he asks for time to think about it. Several days go by, and now it's the first part of the following week and he turns down your offer.

That means you need to approach your second-choice candidate. But along with all of the other applicants, your second choice is wondering why he hasn't heard from you. By now, he is a bit ticked off at you because you haven't kept your word. An extra week has gone by and he hasn't heard from you. He's thinking to himself, *What kind of company is this? I was interested in them but now I'm not too sure because of how they treat their applicants.*

I have heard this scenario countless times from the applicants' point of view, and they never feel warm and fuzzy about the company at this point. Save yourself some possible headaches here and tell potential hires that they can call you if they think of any additional questions they would like answered or they just want a status report. This means there could be some applicants who may call that you won't end up hiring. But I have found that very few people actually take me up on this unless they really do need to reach me.

This practice is a good way to build rapport without much of a drain on your time. It's also helpful with applicants who have received a job offer elsewhere. Instead of losing them, you have opened the door to let them call you and keep you in the game. It's even okay to point-blank ask your top candidates to keep you informed of other offers they may receive.

So you see why it's so important to continue selling during the entire interview process. In a tight labor market, you must move in on good candidates much more quickly than you used to or they will slip away.

THE BATTLE FOR THE BEST

I myself have worked through different labor markets, from double-digit unemployment to the equivalent of zero unemployment. I have done hiring all across the United States and in most industries. At the time this book is published, the labor market will have changed from what it was when I first began writing. Whether we can't find enough qualified applicants to fill our job openings or we have an abundance of applicants, knowing how to select high performers will not become obsolete. Hiring well is not dependent on the labor market; it stands alone. No matter what the labor supply looks like for any industry at any given time, there will always be a battle for the best talent.

If you define a top performer as someone who produces more results, why would you want to choose someone who will produce less? Rarely if ever is this the better option. Regularly some people will disagree with this and defend their challenges by telling me about their work environments and how they are in a state of disarray and are not conducive for a high achiever to achieve. I tell them that is one of the best reasons for hiring a high performer. You shouldn't select the lesser performers while you wait for change to happen. You must begin to upgrade your talent first. It's doubtful that an environment will become more favorable toward achievement without a catalyst of higher achievers to encourage it. Given the choice of passing on a high performer or hiring him, I'll choose every time to surround myself with the best.

ONE FINAL MESSAGE

I want to finish this book with a message to all interviewers but from the more personal standpoint of one person to another. I know this book is about how to identify and hire high performers. It is about motivation, attitude, passion, and ultimately job performance. I would like to leave you with a thought not about interviewing but rather about something more useful for your own personal life.

Now that you know about attitude and passion and how they affect your applicants and your employees, know that they also affect you. Apply the information within this book to yourself. Discover your passion and then know that dreams can be achieved—and that includes *your* dreams.

The unfortunate part is that by the time we learn about locus of control and what it is, our own locus of control is already established and is somewhat entrenched. But that doesn't mean it can't change. It's not impossible to alter your view of how much control you have over your own circumstances. If you don't like where you think your locus of control is, you can change your outlook, your attitude, and how you choose to view life. You have the choice to expand or constrict your thinking. You have the choice to be a positive thinker or a negative one. You can believe you can or you can believe you can't; it is all a choice. And it is a choice that only you have control over. No one has this power over you.

The other piece, besides locus of control, is passion. Know that as long as you are alive, it is never too late to discover yours. The answer to the question "what exactly is my passion?" can be found in only one place, within one's own self. There is no other road that will take you to this answer. But if you get stuck or discouraged, there are many resources and tools available to guide your way. Use them.

Don't allow obstacles to become your excuse for accepting less than your greatest potential. Obstacles are merely gracious opportunities that prepare us for greatness. Obstacles and adversity possess no power themselves; they only have the power that we give them. Don't give them any. They don't have to tear us down or block our way unless we allow them to by quitting first. They are merely learning opportunities that are meant to be conquered, to build us up, and to help us to see the greatness we truly can achieve.

You realize now that anyone can do a good job when it's easy. It's mastering the tough stuff that makes us high performers, not mastering the easy things. Experiencing obstacles and adversity actually helps us to become great. It's when we overcome the roadblocks that we get further than those who throw in the towel and then blame something external for the outcome. It is having the right attitude that gets us through this.

Take the time to rethink how you think. Don't be threatened by this. You will not be able to experience personal growth until you are ready to let go of the attitudes that are holding you back. Once you open yourself up and expand your thinking, then you can grow. And it will be then that you will be able to see the opportunities, ones that you were unable to see before. They are right in front of you, just waiting for you to acknowledge your greatness. Know that all people have great human potential—and that includes you and me!

INDEX

A

achievement, 38

adversity, 35-36, 108, 181

adversity, viewing, 44-45

Apollo 13, 27

applicant information,
    gathering, 69-101

applicant,
    relaxing during an interview,
      73-74
    selling them, 168-173
    leading, 79-81

assessment, factors critical to, 83

attitude change, 23

attitude, 22-28
    assessing, 24
    IQ and, 28

B

bad hire, 165-166
    defining a, 128-131

behavior,
    pattern of, 118
    predominant, 118-127

behavior-based interviewing,
    18-19, 85

C

career fit, 96-97, 131

career paths, 55-57

collaboration, 58-67

compromise, 151-163
    choosing not to, 163

ABOUT THE AUTHOR

As president and founder of Hire Authority, Inc., a company that specializes in training interviewers, Carol Quinn teaches her cutting-edge methodology in workshops all over the United States. Ms. Quinn uses examples based on thousands of actual interviews to demonstrate the practical application of Motivation-Based Interviewing. She appears regularly as a keynote speaker, she has had articles published in *Working Woman* magazine, *Profit* magazine, and many major trade publications, including *Employment Management Today*.